The Falcon And The Moon

by

Catherine Darby

Dales Large Print Books
Long Preston, North Yorkshire,
BD23 4ND, England.

British Library Cataloguing in Publication Data.

Darby, Catherine
    The falcon and the moon.

    A catalogue record of this book is
    available from the British Library

    ISBN   1-84262-228-5 pbk

First published in Great Britain 1977
by Robert Hale & Company

Published in Large Print 2003 by arrangement with
Robert Hale Limited

Dales Large Print is an imprint of Library Magna Books Ltd.

Printed and bound in Great Britain by
T.J. (International) Ltd. Cornwall, PL28

THE FALCONS

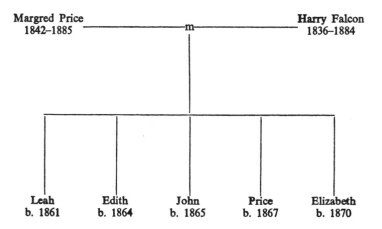

Margred Price
1842–1885 ————————— m ————————— Harry Falcon
                                          1836–1884

Leah   Edith   John   Price   Elizabeth
b. 1861   b. 1864   b. 1865   b. 1867   b. 1870

CHAPTER ONE

1886

Leah Falcon was pleased with herself. The arrangements for the dedication of the stained glass window in the village church had been left in her hands, the vicar being a sensible man who knew when he had met his match in the arts of organization and argument. She had worked hard to ensure that nothing in the ceremony would be wanting in the way of respect to the memory of her parents, and it was known in Marie Regina that, while attendance at the service was voluntary, Miss Leah would notice any absentees.

There would have been none anyway. It was not often that all the Falcons appeared in public together and as it was rumoured that a strain of eccentricity ran through the family then their concerted appearance was an opportunity not to be missed.

'Mind, sir! I'm not saying that any of them was ever bad enough to be confined,' the landlord of the local tavern said earnestly to the gentleman leaning on the bar, 'We've had Falcons here ever since old Harry the Eighth drove the monks out of the monastery, and that's going back a good many years now.'

'About three-hundred and fifty,' the visitor said. 'As you say, sir, and you'd likely know, being educated.' Jake gave his customer a faintly irritated glance. It was like those London newspapers to send down a young fellow who liked to air his knowledge. Not that this Mr Paul Simmons wasn't pleasant enough in his way. He'd paid in advance for his three night's lodging and had already bought his host a couple of rounds. But it didn't do for a jumped up Cockney journalist to wander into Marie Regina and start imagining he knew everything.

'Been here ever since then,' Jake confided. 'Started as plain squires, they did, and worked their way up, so to speak, gathering titles and lands as they went along. Why, one of them was a king's mistress once, so there's Stuart blood in the family for all it's the wrong side of the blanket.'

'And the family now?' Paul Simmons was not much interested in bygone history, 'I take it that the late Lord and Lady Falcon

10

were greatly respected?'

'Lord Harry and Lady Margred,' Jake said. 'That was a real love-match, if ever I saw one. They had eyes for nobody but each other from the day they were wed. Lord Harry now – you couldn't hope to meet a kinder gentleman. Well set up, always ready to pass the time of day – it's a crying shame he was taken so young. Only forty-eight and never a day's illness, and then his horse misjudges a fence and there's milord with a broken neck.'

'You were here?'

'I was called out,' Jake said, 'to help carry him back to the big house. I'll never forget the look on Lady Margred's face when we took him into the big hall. She was a cousin of his, you know. Came from Wales originally and she'd the Welsh lilt in her voice. Tiny woman with black hair and queer amber eyes. I can still see those eyes getting bigger and bigger, and all the colour going out of her face. She took it hard, sir. Quietly, without tears, but hard. It's easier on a woman if she can cry.'

'And she didn't live very long after that, did she?'

'Scarcely a year, sir. She went – not exactly peculiar, but a mite odd. Took to riding around the estate in all weathers. It's my belief she was hoping to go the same way that he went, but in the end she was taken with the consumption and went that way.'

'And the family? There are five of them, I think you said?'

'That's right, sir.' Jake took a pull at his tankard and lowered his voice slightly. It might not be the wisest thing in the world to chatter to a journalist, but the bar was empty and he could not resist the temptation to show off his superior knowledge. 'Miss Leah is the eldest. Twenty-five she is. Very religious young lady.'

Paul Simmons mentally substituted the words 'Old maid,' and nodded encouragement.

'Miss Edith comes next. She's – let me see, Miss Edith will be twenty-two. Then there's Lord John – he took the title after his father died but he only took his seat in the Lords this year when he came of age. Young Mr Price is two years younger and just down from Oxford. And Miss Elizabeth – she's about sixteen, and the baby of the family.'

'And none of them wed?'

The journalist looked mildly surprised, 'They've been in mourning this past year for their mother,' Jake reminded him. 'Oh, Miss

12

Leah and Miss Edith were both presented at Court while Lord Harry was still alive, and we did hear a rumour that Miss Edith was engaged to one of the Stanhopes but nothing came of it. Likely the young gentleman heard of the witch blood.'

'Witch blood?'

'It's an old superstition, full of emptiness, sir.' Jake eyed his tankard.

'Another beer,' Paul Simmons said, taking the hint. 'And have one yourself. It's an uncommonly fine brew.'

'From Falcon hops, sir, and there's no better brew in Kent.'

Jake replenished the two glasses.

'About the witch blood–?'

'An old tale,' Jake said, 'and yet there are those even in this day and age who'll tell you it's true. They say a witch out of Wales married into the family once. There's always been a streak of Welsh in them. Anyway, she had a mark on her to prove she was a witch and from that time on there's always been a female with the same mark born into the family every so often. Mind, it's only a tale, but in these parts you'll still find folk who'll believe anything if it's silly enough. You'll not be putting any of this in your newspaper, will you?'

'No, no. My editor wants only a straight-forward account.'

'I'd not want any trouble,' Jake said with a trace of nervousness. 'Not that I set any store by these things, but there's no denying the Falcons have a strangeness in them. Comes from marrying their cousins too often.'

'I suppose every old family has plenty of skeletons in its closets,' Paul Simmons said, and glanced at his fob-watch.

In a few minutes the Falcons would be arriving for the ceremony. He ought to be making his way across to the church at the other side of the green in the hope of snatching an interview when the service was over. If he made a mess of this assignment he would be looking for a new post within a week. His editor had already intimated that he might be better employed in some career which did not demand that deadlines be met.

'They sound a queer lot,' he said, referring to the Falcons as he calculated there was time for one more drink.

In blissful ignorance of the discussion taking place in the bar, Leah Falcon continued to feel pleased with herself.

Trim in the high-collared black silk gown with its frilled bustle, her brown hair looped

14

in heavy coils under a small, forward tilting hat, she climbed into the carriage. Behind her the ivied façade of the stone house was enclosed within the courtyard walls. This part of Kingsmead had changed not at all since Tudor times, the two back-sweeping wings having been added at later dates. The building had escaped the attentions of Victorian improvers and remained unfashionably simple, its high roof bare of cupolas and gargoyles, its windows twinkling deep in their mullions with no trace of bays or verandahs. She gave her two sisters sharply critical glances as she settled herself opposite them. Both, like herself, wore black, Leah having insisted upon a full twelve-month mourning for their mother. Both were fair-haired, but there the resemblance between them ended. Edith's smooth golden hair was parted in the centre and wound in plaits about her ears. In her pale, exquisitely moulded face Madonna blue eyes were lowered demurely to her mittened hands. Edith looked spiritual and delicate, though in reality she was healthy, optimistic and slightly stupid. Too stupid to catch a husband anyway, Leah thought, for all that Mam had flung her at every eligible male during the London season.

Elizabeth who sat, with equal primness next to Edith, was smaller than her sisters and inclined to plumpness. Her hair, more honey than gold, curled rebelliously about a round, fresh complexioned face. When she smiled her mouth went down slightly at one side, giving her a touch of wry wistfulness. Her eyes were neither blue, nor grey, nor green, but a mixture of all those colours with a broad band of yellow around the irises. They bore their usual expression of faintly dreaming mockery.

'The boys will ride escort,' Leah said.

'Like Royalty,' Edith commented, and giggled.

'Do you have to be so frivolous?' Leah asked, repressively. 'It is after all only a year since poor Mam was taken.'

In Leah's world nobody ever died. They were either taken, passed over or passed on.

'Mam wouldn't have wanted us to be miserable for ever.' Elizabeth said.

'You will kindly allow me to be the judge of what is proper, Beth,' Leah said sharply.

Beth quirked an eyebrow and looked out of the window as the carriage moved off slowly over the cobbles and under the archway to the broad, tree-lined avenue beyond. She knew it was useless to argue with Leah, who had always been perpetually and irritatingly right, but she disagreed all the same. Until Papa's death Mam had been gay and smiling, forever making up games and jokes and singing queer little Welsh songs in the language she had learned as a child and never forgotten. Beth had been Mam's favourite, not that Margred had ever treated any of the children unfairly, but there had been a special bond between her and the youngest. Perhaps, thought Beth, still gazing through the carriage window, it was because she, like Mam, had on her thigh the mark of a purple crescent moon.

'It is the mark of a witch,' Leah had once said in a fit of cold temper.

Beth had run weeping to her Mother, and that was when Margred had lifted her full skirts to show the mark high on her own leg.

'It is a special sign,' she had told Beth, 'borne by very special people. Those who have it hold the future in their own minds, and must never be vain because they know more than other folk.'

Beth only half-understood her mother's words, not at that time connecting the future with those flashes of 'otherness' that sometimes came upon her. But she was always aware of how her mother felt about things.

17

Mam had not laughed or sang again after Papa's death. She had shrunk into herself, and crept about with a frozen look on her face like the stone angel at the entrance to the old Falcon tomb. And just before her own death she had begun to smile again and brush her dark hair as if she were preparing to meet somebody she loved.

And now Leah was declaring that they ought to wear long faces and go around in hideous black!

Beth grimaced inwardly and wondered what Leah would say if she threw back her head and started to sing one of the songs that Mam used to hum before Papa had died and the laughter had gone out of her.

They had turned onto the main road which ran like a broad white ribbon from London to Maidstone. The Falcon estate, with its hop-fields and orchards and golden wheat, stretched along one side of the road. The estate was divided by a river which ran under the wooden bridge spanning the road and divided the land at the other side, separating the village from the high hill crowned by the ruins of the old monastery.

Traffic had become quite heavy on the main road in recent years, and there were continual complaints about the need for a new bridge to replace the old wooden structure, but on this warm, August afternoon the road was empty. Behind the carriage Beth could hear the trotting hoofs of her brothers' mounts.

John and Price were not often at Kingsmead. John preferred his bachelor quarters in London to the quietness of Kingsmead, and Price usually spent his vacations with his brother. In looks both resembled their father, having the same blond-dappled brown hair and wide shoulders, but Price had the slight advantage in height. Beth was fond of them both but preferred Price. John sometimes had a look of Leah about his mouth. They were swinging right down the side road that branched off just before the bridge into the village. Marie Regina lay in a hollow just below the level of the main road. It had changed little through the centuries, its cobbled high street timeworn, its houses shouldering one another down both its sides. The village inn and the village church faced each other across the green. Sunlight glinted from the gold weather-cock on the church tower, and struck fire from the diamond paned windows of the inn.

The church was already full, its benches

and pews crammed with Fiskes, Stones, Whittles and the descendants of other families whose names were repeated over and over again on the headstones in the cemetery that sprawled over the sloping ground behind the church. Bright-cheeked housewives in their Sunday bonnets, labourers in laundered and ironed smocks, small girls with inquisitive eyes and ribbons in their hair, all rustled and stirred as the jangling of harness sounded beyond the open door. Those late-comers who had been unable to find seats stood at the back and pressed closer against the grey stone walls as the Falcons came in.

Leah favoured the congregation with a brief, sweeping glance that took in the fact that Beulah Stone's neckline was cut too low, that Sam Fiske had neglected to polish his boots, and that Mary Stone was pregnant again. Flanked by her brothers she walked slowly to the family pew, corseted back erect, her strong plain face impassive under the small black hat.

Edith, walking with Beth, smiled, lashes fluttering, at the strange young gentleman who stood just within the door. He was, she thought, exceedingly handsome, his dark sideburns glossy, his shirt ornamented with a ruby pin. That the ruby was an inferior garnet, his cuffs slightly frayed, and his shoes too pointed for gentility escaped her notice as his warm brown eyes fell upon her, and he gave the faint start of recognition with which men usually acknowledged her beauty.

She was, Paul Simmons decided, a fancy little piece to find in such an out of the way place. And, if he were not mistaken, those exquisite blue eyes were sending him a coyly flirtatious message.

The younger girl at her side was also staring at him. Paul wondered what had happened to give her that blank, shocked expression as if she looked beyond him to something only she could see.

Then both girls lowered their eyes and paced sedately after their elders as the minister, resplendent in his Sunday surplice, came in and the organ swelled into a hymn.

It was, thought Price, opening his mouth and adding his strong baritone to the congregation's vocal efforts, a bit of a bore to be dragged back from a pleasant boating vacation in order to attend a dedication ceremony. There was also the little high-stepper he'd just installed in a snug Bayswater apartment. She was an extravagant puss, but fortunately, his allowance under the terms of his father's Will was a generous one. But it was an annoyance to have to kick one's heels in this hole for the best part of a week, simply because Leah had a bee in her bonnet about the family's setting an example to everybody else.

John, flanking Leah, slanted a look towards the shrouded window and hoped he had done right in leaving its design to her. His sister had the same classical, faintly severe tastes as himself, but one could never be quite certain about females. Yet Leah was generally reliable. She had more or less managed the household since Papa's death. Certainly Mam had been very little use. John, who had disapproved of his mother almost as much as he had loved her, sighed briefly. There was no denying that Mam, with her flying black hair and husky laugh, had been something of an embarrassment, but there were times when her absence struck him with a pang of loneliness.

Edith, watching as her brother moved to tug the cord that would unveil the memorial window, longed to turn her head to see if the strange gentleman was still gazing at her. It would, however, be unladylike to reveal her own interest in him, so she kept her eyes fixed upon John.

The curtain parted and the stained glass blazed into the greyness of the church as a shaft of sunlight glowed through it in a tunnel of bright gold and little, dancing motes of dust.

Leah's taste had not faltered. An out-stretched falcon hovered over tiny blossoms circling a plump cherub. The colours of red and blue and gold blended into a harmony of pattern.

There were ripples of interest and approval as those at the back craned their necks to see. Mr Allen, the minister, smiled benignly as John resumed his seat, and then rose to give the brief address he had prepared.

Paul Simmons, resting his notebook against the side of the font scribbled busily. 'A fine old Kentish family with a dash of Celtic blood. Sir Harry a tower of strength in the community. Lady Margred noted for her grace and charm. Their early deaths a tragedy, yet, in death they were now undivided.'

Not a word about witch marks or witch blood. Why the devil had that girl stared at him in such a fashion? Beth, gazing at the bright mosaic of coloured glass, shivered as the numbness drained out of her. It had happened as she glanced at the stranger – a sudden terror as if a pit had opened and she was looking down into unimaginable depths. The fear had not been for herself but for Edith and, in a queer way, for Leah too. It was as if some danger threatened both her sisters, and then had come the cold, sick feeling as if part of her were in the church and the other part of her struggling through a heavy mist in a place she couldn't recognize. It had been a long time since a similar event had made her teeth chatter and the colour forsake her cheeks. It had been when Papa was still alive, and he had taken her to see his new bay mare.

'Gentle as a babe!' he had exclaimed, running his hand over the gleaming coat as the mare nuzzled him in the hope of sugar.

And Beth had stood there with the black terror sweeping over her, and not remembering it again until two years later when some men from the village had carried Papa home and spoken of a high hedge, of the bay mare's stumbling, of a jagged stone in the road that might have caused the accident.

Always for the other people, never for herself. She had to live each day as it came, but if she looked at another person very hard, not with her eyes but with her mind, she could often see events in their lives unroll like pictures in a magic lantern show.

Edith poked her and she stood to sing the closing hymn, her voice wobbling as usual between the notes. When she was alone she could sing quite prettily, but when other folk were around her throat closed up and the tune came out wrong.

The Falcons came out of the church first, as if they were Royalty, and stood outside exchanging greetings with the rest of the villagers. Caps were pulled, curtseys dropped, hands shaken, enquiries made as to crops and children. Mr Allen, divested of his surplice, received congratulations on his address from Leah.

'My parents would be most gratified to hear themselves spoken of with such appreciation,' she said.

'They are a sad loss to the community,' Mr Allen agreed. Leah's brows rushed together in a slight frown.

'Naturally my brother will be taking over most of the running of the estate now that he has entered his majority,' she said. 'We must not eulogize the dead at the expense of the living.'

'Of course not – it was never my intention to imply, Lord John is sadly missed when he is in London,' Mr Allen said hastily.

Mollified, Leah awarded him a small, forgiving smile and turned to see the strange gentleman who had been standing at the back of the church. She nodded in brief acknowledgement of his bow, and was startled when he moved forward to speak to her.

'Miss Leah Falcon? Paul Simmons, ma'am, of the *Daily Recorder*. I'm here to write up this afternoon's occasion for my newspaper.'

She might have guessed he was a journalist. He had the faintly seedy look she associated with persons of that class. His voice was pleasant however and his manner respectful.

Her own manner softened imperceptibly as she replied, 'This is not a matter of great public interest, sir, merely a small, family affair. We are not seekers after publicity, you know.'

'But a human interest story,' he countered, 'makes a refreshing change for our readers.'

Leah's politeness sharpened into faint alarm. Although scandal had lain dormant for more than a quarter of a century she was well aware that it would require very little digging for a great number of reprehensible facts about her forbears to be unearthed. The thought of having them blazoned over the smudged pages of a London newspaper made her shudder.

'If you would care for a personal interview,' she said swiftly, 'perhaps you would call upon me – shall we say tomorrow at eleven? I will be happy to check the facts in your article.'

She gave him a gracious little bow before stepping up into the carriage. Her air of regal patronage would have been amusing in a prettier woman, but in her it seemed right.

Paul stepped back, watching as the younger girls followed. The blue-eyed one hesitated, giving him another long, fluttering glance. The smallest girl gave him a brief, incurious stare with no trace in it of the blank terror she had previously shown.

The villagers remained to gossip and to admire the new window. Afternoon sunshine lay like a golden pall over Marie Regina.

CHAPTER TWO

Paul Simmons walked up from the village the next morning. The air helped to dissipate the headache with which he had awoken after a hard night's drinking in the bar. He had a vague recollection of having heard some interesting titbits about the Falcons, but had neglected to make any notes.

The gates of Kingsmead stood open and the drive wound ahead between oak and elm, with meadows stretching beyond the trees. It was not, at a thousand acres, an enormous estate but compared with the mean tenement where Paul had spent his formative years it was a Paradise. He walked slowly, savouring the light breeze, the soft hues of the landscape. In such a place a man had room to breathe, time in which to do the things that were congenial. More important a man living here would have money. Remembering his unpublished novel Paul sighed. It would cost more than a hundred pounds to publish the book at his own expense, no publisher being willing to launch him. It might as well be a thousand pounds!

He had reached an archway set in a high wall, through which he could see a cobbled yard and the façade of a handsome manor. As he walked up to the shallow flight of steps leading to the main door, the heavy oak was pulled open from within and the blue-eyed girl stood on the threshold.

This morning she had discarded her black

for a blue gown, its ruffles caught back over a small bustle, its high collar and tight cuffs lace edged. Her gilt coils of hair were ornamented with tiny blue bows, and her manner was both flustered and welcoming.

'It's Mr Simmons, isn't it? Leah, my sister, asked me to entertain you until she returned. She was called over to Mrs Whittle's Edna. The silly girl decided it would be fun to swallow some pins – Edna, I mean, not my sister. So Leah was sent for to make Edna swallow some bread. And would you like to take a cup of coffee?'

He wondered briefly why she had opened the door herself, instead of waiting for a maidservant to announce him. She gave the impression of having rushed down, for fear some opportunity might be missed.

Then he forgot about her as he stepped into a high raftered hall that stretched up through two storeys. At the far end twin fireplaces were set at each side of a stone staircase that led to a broad, railed gallery. No carpet muffled the flagstones but tapestries, so faded that their pattern was almost lost, shrouded the walls. Along one of these walls stood a trestle table with high-backed chairs ranged about it, and, opposite, an enormous dresser crammed with silver ware and pewter towered up.

'Pure Gothic,' he exclaimed.

'Is it?' Edith sounded uninterested. 'It used to be the old family hall. Leah thinks it's beautiful and won't have anything changed. I think it's quite hideous. Would you like to come into the drawing-room? We can have some coffee or do you like madeira?'

'Coffee would be fine.' He felt slightly queasy at the thought of more alcohol.

She preceded him through a door on the left and turned right into a long, light room with floor length windows that looked out over green lawns to the beginnings of parkland. Its walnut panelling was late seventeenth century, Paul decided, and some tasteful hand had furnished it in shades of rose and apricot.

'Is this Gothic?' Edith enquired, seating herself at a small table and ringing a handbell vigorously.

'No, indeed. This is late Restoration and almost perfectly in period.'

'Yes, it has been restored quite a lot,' Edith said brightly. 'The rooms through there,' she pointed towards the front of the house, 'are just as they were in Tudor times, except for some panelling that was done later on. Leah won't have anything in them changed. She even insists on using the old names – solar and parlour. Too bourgeois! Oh, Annie, will you bring coffee and some wafer biscuits? Cook made some yesterday, I believe.'

The rosy-cheeked maid, who had arrived in answer to the bell, said stolidly,

'If you please, Miss Edith, but Miss Beth ate the last of the wafers yesterday, and Cook's not got round to making a fresh batch.'

'Then bring the coffee. My sister,' Edith said, as the maid withdrew, 'is forever nibbling between meals! Of course she is not "out" yet, but that doesn't excuse greediness.'

'I take it that you have had your London season?'

'Yes.' Her lovely face clouded briefly as if at some painful memory. 'When I was eighteen, Leah and I were presented together. We had never been to London before and it was all very gay. Balls and theatre visits and new dresses, you know. Mam and Papa took a house in London, and we met some very nice people.'

He wondered that neither she nor her sister had found husbands. Edith Falcon was a beauty and Leah, although she was not pretty, had elegance. The family was an

31

old established one and, by his standards, wealthy. By now both the young ladies ought to be safely settled.

'Do you go up to town much these days?' he enquired. 'Not at all.' Her mouth had a discontented droop. 'My parents were never happy away from Kingsmead for very long, and then Papa was killed and Mam died – these past two years we have not been out of mourning. What did you think of the service yesterday?'

'Very fitting and dignified.'

'Leah arranged it,' Edith informed him. 'Leah arranges everything, you know. Price says that the first thing she'll do if she gets to heaven is sort out all the angels and then spring clean the place.'

She gave a sudden gurgle of laughter, as the maid came in again with coffee.

Paul, watching Edith pour the fragrant beverage, was fascinated by her slow grace, by the white wrists from which the lace cuffs fell away. She made a little ritual of the ceremony as if she were playing at being hostess. As she handed his cup, her blue eyes held his a fraction longer than was necessary and were veiled by her lashes again.

'Did I understand your sister to say that Lord Falcon would be at home from now on?' Paul asked.

'Lord? – oh, you mean John! Yes, now that he's of age, Leah thinks he ought to devote more time to the estate. Of course he will still have to take his seat in the Lords from time to time. And I suppose Price will help to manage the land. Leah wants it.'

'It's a large property,' he commented.

'Only a thousand acres,' Edith shrugged. 'We all of us live at Kingsmead mainly, but we have a farm at the other side of the monastery ruins and a house in Maidstone. Those are rented out. We used to have another house at the other side of the river, but it was burned down years and years ago. Mam was always talking about having it rebuilt and used as a school for orphan children, but nothing was ever done. Are you going to write all this in your newspaper, Mr Simmons?'

'Newspaper?' He had forgotten his article had pushed his imminent return to London to the back of his mind. It was infinitely more pleasant to sit in this elegant room, talking to this lovely girl and sipping coffee as if he were a guest. 'Oh, my article! That will contain nothing disrespectful, I assure you.'

'Leah will make certain of that,' Edith said. 'She doesn't like gossip about the family, and she doesn't like us to do anything to cause gossip. She says we have a duty to set an example to the neighbours.'

'And have the Falcons always set an example?' he ventured.

'Lord, no!' Her eyes sparkled with amusement. 'In the past our family has had more than its share of rogues. Come with me, and I'll show you something.'

She rose and swished ahead of him back into the great hall and began to mount the staircase.

'The family portraits are all hung along the wall,' she said over her shoulder. 'All the masters of Kingsmead and their wives, right back to the first Harry Falcon. And they weren't all respectable. That one betrayed his own brother's wife!'

She nodded towards a florid gentleman in plumed hat and brocade coat.

'And that is Lady Regina Falcon,' Edith chattered on. 'She was a king's mistress, you know. King Charles the Second. Of course he had a great many lady friends, and I don't suppose she was one of the most important, but she bore the king a son and this is how a peerage came into the family. And this is that son. They say he used to drink blood, but I'm not sure if I believe that.'

'I'm not sure I believe it either,' Paul said. 'This is Mam.' Edith had paused and a sadness came into her face. 'She was very pretty before Papa was killed. Leah and John thought she ought to have behaved more sedately, but she laughed at them and went her own way.'

The small, vivid face glowed out of the canvas, the slanting eyes warm amber, the black hair coiled around the ears, slender neck rising from a fichu of creamy lace.

'Did you know she was Papa's second wife?' Edith enquired.

'No, no, I didn't.'

'And grandfather was married twice too. His second wife was Papa's stepmother. Her name was Willow, and they say she died "by act of God".'

'What does that mean?'

'I'm sure I don't know. Probably struck by lightning,' Edith said cheerfully. 'But she had time to curse the family before she died, so it might not have been lightning.'

'A curse?'

'Well, not exactly a curse,' Edith said doubtfully. 'But she did say "Victory will not come until a Falcon rides upon a moth." Mam told us about it when we were quite little. Of course it all happened years ago before she and Papa were wed. His first wife died young. It's odd isn't it, that both Papa and Grandfather should have been married twice, and yet none of us is wed.'

'But there is surely plenty of time,' Paul said gallantly. 'Young ladies, so I'm informed, like to pick and choose.'

'When there is choice,' Edith said, and the discontent had returned to her voice. 'There is absolutely nobody worth meeting in Marie Regina. Leah never considers that, of course. She would be quite happy to bury herself and everybody else at Kingsmead for ever. And this house is like a museum. She will not allow anything to be changed.'

'But surely the property belongs to your brother?' Paul queried.

'To John, yes. All of it is his, except for the cottage that Mam left to Beth. But John and Leah have always agreed together on everything.'

From the hall below brisk footsteps sounded and Leah's voice rose up clearly,

'Edith! Edith, did that young man arrive?'

'We're up here,' Edith called back. Her face had fallen slightly at the sound of her sister's voice.

'Oh, are you showing him the portraits?'

Leah began to mount the stairs towards

them. She too had taken off mourning, but her basqued dress was of sombre purple and a black snood encased her hair. Her glance, flickering towards Edith, disapproved.

'Pale blue, so soon?' she queried.

'Purple doesn't suit me,' Edith said flippantly.

'Miss Edith was kind enough to show me some of your forbears,' Paul bowed.

'I hardly think the doings of my ancestors will be of much interest to the readers of your newspaper,' Leah said.

'On the contrary,' Paul said. 'My readers are avid for titbits of information about the quality.'

'I've no doubt,' Leah said icily, 'but it is not incumbent on us to provide them with such information. Would you like to come down into the drawing-room, and we will discuss the form that your article might take?'

She was already leading the way down-stairs, her back stiffly erect, her thin hands clenched against her skirt.

Edith raised her eyebrows at Paul and followed, her attitude defiantly jaunty as if she were a small girl caught out in some mischief.

In the drawing-room Leah seated herself on the edge of a high-backed chair, and nodded a dismissal towards her sister.

'Edith, go and see if you can find Beth. The silly child has neither practised her pianoforte nor completed that watercolour she began,' she said.

'I think Beth went over to "Witch's Dower",' Edith said.

'Then you'd better go and see if you can help Cook with the week's menus,' Leah said.

'But I don't see why I have to go now.'

'Because Cook wishes to know what to prepare. Surely you are capable of drawing up a few simple family menus without my help! You can't expect me to see to everything.'

'I thought that *you* expected it,' Edith said with a flash of temper, but she left the room nonetheless.

'Edith is very young for her years,' Leah said excusingly. 'She has had very little experience of the world.'

'Apart from her London season?'

'We both had a London season,' Leah said gently. 'It was an exceedingly expensive waste of time. I disliked the bustle of the city and was only too pleased to come home.'

'"Witch's Dower",' Paul said thoughtfully. 'That's a most unusual name.'

'It's a local name the villagers give to a small cottage down by the river,' Leah said. 'It was my mother's property and she left it to Beth. The child spends altogether too much time down there.'

He remembered Jake's words concerning witch blood, and would have liked to enquire further, but Leah was speaking again, her face and tone businesslike.

'You have, I assume, made notes for this article?'

'Yes, indeed.'

'You had better let me see them.'

She stretched out her hand with calm authority.

Paul fumbled in his pocket, brought out his small notebook and gave it to her meekly.

'But these are squiggles!' she exclaimed a moment later.

'My own brand of shorthand writing, Miss Leah.' She closed the book with a little snap and gave it back to him.

'You had better call back tomorrow,' she said, 'and let me read through your first draft. I can check it for any inaccuracies.'

'It is hardly usual–'

'And you need not include in your account anything concerning my forbears. A simple, dignified account of yesterday's ceremony, a few words concerning the services rendered to the district by my father and grandfather.'

'The two gentlemen who each married twice? Your sister was talking of an act of God.'

'Edith talks a great deal of nonsense,' Leah frowned. 'My grandfather's first wife died when Papa was born, and Papa was reared by his stepmother, Willow. Papa's own first wife and Lady Willow were both killed in the same instant, most tragically.'

'An accident?'

'An old tree that used to stand outside the courtyard was uprooted during a storm and fell on them,' Leah said. 'That was the "act of God" my sister babbled about. Shortly afterwards Papa wed my mother. Their lives were both very happy, but cut short too soon.'

'Yes, indeed.'

'But you will not be returning to London immediately, will you?' Her manner was a shade more friendly.

'In a day or two, I must,' Paul said. 'My editor expects this by the end of the week, and he is a difficult gentleman to please.'

'You sound as if you do not find your employment congenial,' Leah said.

'It is a means of earning my living until I

can make shift to have my novel published.'

'You have written a novel?'

'Yes, Miss Leah. I am vain enough to believe the book has merit, but so far I have not found a publisher to agree with me. The general opinion seems to be that my book does not fit the present trend of public taste.'

'And public taste is deplorable at the present time. Nothing but yellow backed novels and sentimental poetry. Can you not publish the book yourself?'

'It's an expensive process,' Paul said ruefully.

'And journalism is not, I imagine, a lucrative profession,' Leah sounded sympathetic.

'It is a bare living,' Paul said and, hearing the note of self-pity in his voice, added hastily, 'But occasionally one gets an assignment out of town, and the opportunity to meet some cultured people.'

'You do not disapprove of blue-stockings then?' She sounded almost arch.

'On the contrary,' he said earnestly, 'I enjoy the company of an intelligent woman. Books, music, art are surely to be enjoyed by both sexes.'

'When duty permits.'

As if mindful of her own obligations she glanced at the gold fob-watch pinned to her bodice and rose. The audience, he thought with a spasm of amusement, was at an end.

As he crossed the main hall he was struck again by its ageless quality. It had a grace in its shabbiness, an honesty, that no modern décor could emulate. He was conscious of the generations that had trodden the flagstones. He could trace his own family back only to his grandfather, a printer by trade who had died in debt, and handed down to his grandson only a love of words, a craving for the scent of fresh print on white paper, and the urge to be something better than he was without working too hard.

Edith had come to a baize covered door on the right at the same instant that Leah came to the door at the left. Glancing back as the maid opened the front door, Paul saw both the sisters, poised like alternative choices at each side, Leah in her sombre purple with the eager look in her fine eyes, and Edith with a ridiculous apron tied about her blue dress.

Then the door closed behind him and he went slowly down the steps into the courtyard again. The morning was still fine, the breeze a little fresher, and his headache had gone.

He pictured himself striding across his own

property, rifle in his hand, a couple of gun-dogs at his heels. A far cry from tenements and cheap lodgings and the hustle of Fleet Street.

An old childhood fantasy swept over him. His parents were not his real parents at all, but a couple who had taken him in as a foundling not knowing him to be the son of an earl. Or perhaps he had a dash of foreign blood, something rich and exotic that would explain his craving for beauty, his feeling that he did not belong in the world where he had been reared.

He became aware that he had strayed from the main drive and was walking a sloping meadow, starred with small flowers. The turf under his thin soled shoes was springy, the sky above clear.

'Bring back everything you can dig up on the Falcons,' his editor had ordered. 'If it's good, we'll give you a by-line and make it a main feature. If you fall down on this one, so help me I'll see you never work in Fleet Street again.'

The *Daily Recorder* had recently enjoyed increased circulation and a couple of libel actions after a series entitled Vices Of An Aristocrat. The public appetite for scandal had been whetted, and a racy article about a

43

family whose members died 'by act of God' might very well bring him recognition in the shape of an increased salary and a chance to write what he wanted to write.

But that was only a short view. Paul believed in the long term view, which might be less spectacular, but often brought greater rewards. A man would be a fool to write about Kingsmead, when with a little contriving he might live there.

He thought again of the two sisters. Edith Falcon was undoubtedly attracted to him, though he suspected she would have been equally attracted to any personable young man. Her glance had been tender, her figure ripely alluring. On the other hand Leah Falcon had a certain style and she had seemed interested in his novel.

'Good morning! Did you know you were trespassing?'

The girl appeared so suddenly as if she had risen out of the ground, and her dress was the same colour as the grass, its skirt ending above her ankles, its bodice softened by a white collar. In one hand she swung a Leghorn hat trimmed with green ribbon, and her round face was lit with curiosity.

'It's the youngest Miss Falcon, isn't it?'

Startled out of his reverie he remembered

her blankly terrified look of the previous day.

'I'm Beth Falcon, and you're the gentleman who is going to write an article about us. We saw you yesterday at the church.'

'Paul Simmons of the *Daily Recorder*.'

He bowed and she laughed, her smile a trifle crooked, her nose wrinkling. She had neither Leah's elegance nor Edith's beauty, but a strangely wistful charm of her own.

'Are you exploring?' she enquired. 'Would you like me to show you my property?'

'The cottage?'

'Witch's Dower – though Leah doesn't like it to be called thus. Mam left the place to me, you know, and I may invite whom I please there. Will you come?'

She didn't wait for an answer but ran ahead of him across the meadow towards a patch of thick woodland that sloped gently towards the river. In a moment her small, plumpish figure had merged into the shifting greens of the trees.

Paul hurried after her, stumbling a little on the unfamiliar path that twisted and turned and came out abruptly into a clearing.

He was at the back of a small, white-washed house, and there was no sign of Beth Falcon, but as he went round to the front he saw her standing at the half-open door.

CHAPTER THREE

'It's a very old house,' she said, 'nearly as old as Kingsmead. It was built as a dower house for the widow of the owner of Kingsmead, but later on the first Falcon Witch came to live here, and since then it's been passed down through the women in the family. Mam left it to me.'

He had been going to ask why neither of the older sisters had inherited it, but at that same moment he realized that neither of them would have fitted into this setting. Beth, however, looked as if she and the little white house belonged together.

'Would you like to come inside?' she invited.

He bent beneath the lintel and found himself in a long, low room with windows at back and front and a narrow staircase. The room was simply furnished with a few dark pieces which he guessed were very old. A fire was laid but not lit, a grandmother clock ticked in the corner, and there were several pieces of faded and beautiful tapestry.

'There are two bedrooms upstairs,' Beth told him, 'but Leah would be very shocked if I took you to see them.'

'But you don't live here?'

'No, I wish I did! It would be much more fun than being stuck in the big house!' Beth said energetically. 'But I shall live here when I am old enough to please myself. Meanwhile I keep it clean myself and visit it whenever I can. It likes to be visited.'

'Does it?' He hid his amusement but her face was earnest.

'Some houses like to be visited,' she said gravely. 'If they are neglected they grow sick and shabby like folk who are unloved. So I come here nearly every day, and polish and clean and sweep.'

'Isn't it lonely?' he asked curiously.

'Oh no, indeed,' she said. 'If there are ghosts here they are very friendly ones. And the villagers never come here. Would you like to see my favourite room?'

'Yes, indeed.'

Half humouring her, half mystified, Paul watched her push open a door at the foot of the narrow staircase and step into a room beyond.

He followed, pausing on the threshold with a feeling of disappointment. The

47

whitewashed apartment, with windows only at the front, seemed unfurnished save for a long table and a couple of stools. A carved chest stood against the back wall and some curiously shaped bowls and goblets were arranged on shelves in an alcove.

'Can you smell the past?' Beth asked softly. 'Can you smell it all around us?'

He could smell nothing but lavender and cloves, but she stood very still, a listening look on her face.

'This was the herb-room,' she said. 'Long years ago the women who lived in this house brewed potions and wove strange spells. It would be odd, wouldn't it, if they all came back and we could see them?'

For an unknown reason he shivered as if thin, cold fingers had brushed his cheek.

'How many have owned this cottage?' he asked, and his voice was too loud in the room.

'The first Falcon widow – I can't remember her name, and after her the first of the witches, though Leah says all that is nonsense too. But she left the place to her great-granddaughter, Regina–'

'The King's mistress?'

'And she left it to her own granddaughter, Rosemary Falcon. Rosemary never wed, but

48

she left the place to her niece – or it might have been great-niece Apple and Apple gave it to her sister Eliza, and Eliza gave it – to Willow Clegg, I think. She was Papa's stepmother and a sort of cousin.'

'And died "by act of God".'

'Yes, poor dear! A tree fell on her and she was squashed flat. Absolutely flat!' Beth said with relish. 'That was years and years ago, of course. Mam owned the house then and when she died it became mine.'

Regina, Rosemary, Apple, Willow, and others whose names he didn't know. The names were beads strung on a chain of years.

'Why is this your favourite room?' he asked. 'Is it because of the spells and potions?'

'I keep my most prized possessions here,' she said solemnly.

'Oh?'

'Would you like to see them?' she asked. 'I don't show them to many people, but I wouldn't mind your looking at them, if you promise not to smile.'

'Of course not.'

He thought that she was very young for her years as she went to the high shelves and lifted down two objects, one shrouded in black velvet, the other in a leather bag.

She put them both on the table, undid the

drawstrings of the bag, and drew out a small bottle half filled with greyish powder.

'What is it?' he enquired. 'Dragon's blood?'

'It's mandrake powder,' she said, with a hint of reproach, 'You know what a mandrake is, don't you?'

'A root of some kind.'

'A magical root. It shrieks as it's pulled from the earth, you know. And the person who pulls it up generally drops dead.'

She evidently had a taste for horrors, for her voice was cheerfully matter-of-fact.

'One of the Falcon women owned this one, but it shrivelled up and fell into dust. I put it into this bottle.'

'But why?'

'I thought it might come in useful some time,' Beth said vaguely, putting the bottle away. 'Mam told me about it. She knew a lot of interesting things. Sometimes, when I was little, she would bring me here in an afternoon and tell me stories and sing songs. Just the two of us with the shadows growing long across the floor. They were good times.'

She sounded lonely and Paul felt embarrassed pity stirring in him.

'And the other?' He indicated the black velvet.

'This belonged to Mam. When she was a

girl she lived up in Wales on a farm. A gypsy woman gave her this, and she gave it to me.'

It was a crystal ball such as he had seen at fairgrounds, tiny flashes of light darting from within its solid centre.

'I saw some gypsies camped over on the heath as the train was drawing in,' Paul remarked.

'They come every summer,' Beth said. 'There was a time when they stopped coming. One of them committed some crime – I don't know what, but the gypsies didn't come. Then Mam married Papa, and they began to come here again.'

'And what of the crystal, Miss Beth?' he asked teasingly. 'Can you tell fortunes with it? Can you tell mine?'

'Perhaps.' She bit her lip and glanced at him doubtfully. 'Sometimes things don't come through very clearly. I don't do it very often, in case Leah finds out.'

'Try anyway,' he invited.

She took up the crystal and seated herself on one of the stools, indicating that he was to pull up the other one.

As she bent over her long tail of curly hair shadowed the globe. She was so serious that he kept from laughing but there was a stillness in her that drained the amusement out of him.

Between her hands the crystal grew opaque, as if milk had flooded it. Then as it cleared again she began to talk, her voice a sing-song monotone, her eyes fixed on the globe.

'I see a narrow house squeezed between other houses with a yard behind and a high brick wall. There is a tree in the yard, a sooty tree with spindle branches.'

'My house where I grew up,' he murmured, but she went on unheeding.

'And there are three ladies, all weeping, with their faces hidden. One of them has red hair, piled up in curls on her head. She is weeping too, or perhaps she is laughing. It's hard to tell. And over their heads is a silver sword. And now it's all fading, all fading.'

She raised her head slowly, the amber flecks in her eyes gleaming, her round face quite blank.

'It wasn't a very exciting fortune, was it?' she apologized. 'Perhaps I ought to practise more, do you think?'

'I think your sister is right. You ought to leave such things alone,' he said more sharply than he had intended.

Unoffended, Beth got up and returned the crystal to its velvet shroud. Her face wore its apparently normal cheerfulness as she stretched up to replace crystal and mandrake powder on the shelf.

'I ought to offer you something to drink,' she said, 'but I don't keep anything here.'

'I had some coffee up at Kingsmead. Miss Edith was kind enough—'

'I thought Edith would contrive to entertain you,' she interrupted. 'My sister is in hopes of a husband, you know. If a young man comes to Marie Regina she gets all of a flutter! Oh, you mustn't think I'm mocking her. I wish Edith could find a husband, for she's very pretty and very sweet tempered. She and Leah had a season in London, you know, and we all thought that Edith would marry Lord Stanhope, but nothing came of it.'

'And will you have a season in London?' he enquired.

'I don't think so.' She sounded disappointed but resigned. 'Leah would have to chaperone me, you see, and she dislikes going into society. She disapproves of the Prince of Wales, you know, and considers his set is very fast – not that she knows much about it, but Price gets a bit squiffy sometimes and lets things out.'

'Your brother John – doesn't?' he probed.

'Let things out or get squiffy?' She giggled. 'John never does anything wrong. He's so terribly good that he'll probably go straight up to heaven when he dies. He and Leah are both very proper. Would you like me to have another look in the crystal for you? It might be better this time because I'm getting more in the mood.'

'No, thank you.'

He felt a definite antipathy towards the velvet-shrouded, transparent globe.

'Then we'd better go. I'm not supposed to come down here too often. Leah thinks girls ought to spend their days being useful.'

'And don't you want to be useful?' he enquired, following her out to the front door.

'I'm not certain what I want to be,' she said simply. 'I want to be tremendously noble sometimes and go off to convert the heathen, and sometimes I want to be very beautiful and very wicked and have lovers.'

'Who will come riding on white horses through the wood?'

He spoke teasingly, seeking to ingratiate himself into her half-child, half-woman nature, but she answered dreamily as if she were thinking aloud.

'In the end I believe one man will come,

perhaps not on a white horse, but I will know him when he comes and he will know me, and there will never be anybody else for both of us.'

'Beth? Beth, is that you?' Leah's clear, high voice sounded among the trees, and a few seconds later she trotted into the clearing, mounted on a sleek grey mare.

'I met Mr Simmons on his way back to the village,' Beth said. 'I asked him to come and look at the cottage.'

'Mr Simmons is a busy gentleman,' Leah said crossly. 'You have no right to take up his time, and no business at all to be wandering about here when there are tasks to be done at the house. You'd best ride double with me. And put on your hat or you'll be as brown as an Indian!'

'I fear that I must take part of the blame,' Paul said swiftly. 'Miss Beth was doing her best to entertain me, and I neglected to remind her that she might be needed at home.'

'Beth is altogether too forward,' Leah said repressively, leaning to pull her sister up to the saddle. 'You will imagine we are manner-less rustics.'

'Not in the least,' he bowed.

'Leah, aren't you going to invite Mr

Simmons to supper this evening?' Beth asked. 'If he's going to write about the memorial window–'

'I wouldn't dream of intruding on a family affair,' Paul began, but Leah interrupted him, her voice and manner grudging.

'It is not, strictly speaking, a family affair, only a gathering of a few friends and neighbours to mark the occasion. We have supper at eight, so do join us, if your time permits.'

It was obvious that she expected him to refuse, but some imp of perversity made him reply,

'That's uncommonly civil of you, Miss Falcon. I shall be very pleased to accept.'

'Not at all. Tonight, at seven-thirty then?'

Leah smiled and brought down her crop with such vigour that the mare bounded forward with surprise.

Miss Leah, Paul thought as he stood looking after them, would be a handful to tame. He had the perception to realize that she was a more interesting character than her sister Edith, but the younger woman's delicate beauty fascinated him.

It seemed that this was to be a morning of meeting the Falcons. As he wound his way along the narrow bridle path that rose up to the level of the main road, he heard the clattering of hoofs and, as he mounted the steep bank, Price Falcon drew rein a few yards distant and grinned at him amiably.

''Morning! You're the reporter fellow, aren't you? My sister mentioned that you were at the "do" yesterday. Pretty feudal, wasn't it?'

'Pretty feudal.' Paul agreed cautiously.

'They like it, you know,' Price said, dismounting. 'John and Leah, I mean. They enjoyed the bowing and scraping and forelock touching.'

'And you don't?'

'I can take it or leave it,' Price said with the carelessness of one born to privilege. 'Frankly, country life bores me – except for the shooting. Do you shoot?'

'Not often.' Paul though wryly of the target practice he had put in with a catapult on the alley-cats of his boyhood.

'It's a ripping sport,' Price said with enthusiasm. 'Only thing worth bothering about in the country.'

'You live in town?'

'I've apartments there – had them since I came down from Oxford three months ago. I was supposed to get a degree but I flunked second-year, and Leah decided I was wasting my time and ordered me home. Mind, she was quite right. I never did have much in the way of brains.'

But his manner was engaging. There was in the tall youngster something of the boisterous good-nature of a puppy. His brown hair was dappled with gold, his smile was frank, inviting friendship.

'Will you be permanently at Kingsmead now?' Paul asked.

They had begun to stroll without conscious intent along the road together.

'I'll be here when it suits me,' Price said, 'but I'll keep up my town place. Fortunately I got my allowance when I was eighteen, and neither John nor Leah can touch it. John has the whole estate, of course, but none of us were left short, though the girls don't get to control their own money until they're twenty-five. Leah was twenty-five last March so she's independent now, but Edith and Beth will have to wait.'

'But your sister has the cottage?'

'That old place!' Price cast an amused glance back towards the woods. 'Mam left that to Beth. It's of no use to anybody else, but my sister likes it. She's an odd creature full of whims and fancies, but there's more to her than meets the eye.'

58

'I can believe it.'

'I'd best be making tracks for home,' Price said. 'Leah wants the midday meal out of the way so she can start getting everything ready for the supper tonight. By the way, would you like to come?'

'Miss Leah has already invited me,' Paul said, with a small feeling of triumph.

'Lord! She must be in a melting mood!' Price exclaimed. 'She hasn't a good word to say usually for reporters – oh, excuse me!'

'A lot of people haven't a good word to say for reporters.' Paul told him. 'But by profession I'm actually a novelist.'

'Are you, by jove!' The younger man pursed his lips in an ingenuous whistle of admiration. 'You know, I've often thought I'd like to write a book. Turned out one or two rather good essays when I was at Cambridge, as a matter of fact. See you this evening then.'

He swung himself back into the saddle and cantered off, while Paul retraced his steps towards the village.

His interest in the Falcons had driven all thoughts of the proposed article out of his head. He felt he had gained a foothold in a new and enchanted world. Always before he had been on the outside craning his neck to see the society beauties at Goodwood, pushing his way into the Law Courts to take notes on the latest scandal, but never really part of it. Now, suddenly, he was on what might be considered friendly terms with a family that could count itself at least among the lower reaches of the aristocracy.

And of the three unmarried daughters, only Leah had control of her own money. As he strolled along the cobbled street towards the inn, he pictured Leah Falcon. She was a plain woman, but her figure was good and there was something beneath her cool, quiet exterior that interested him. He wondered what it would be like to tame such a woman, to make her fall in love with him. The thought was exciting.

And, after marriage, there would be no more need to rush about, scribbling in a notebook, desperately trying to colour the record of an occasion in brilliant phrases. He could have the leisure to live as gentlemen lived, the money with which to publish his novel.

He ordered mutton pie and a pint of ale from the landlord when he reached the inn, and went through into the small parlour. There was a sprinkling of locals in the saloon bar and so, Jake being occupied, the meal was served by one of the maids.

It suited Paul to be alone for a while. He was aware that an opportunity lay within his grasp, but how was he to secure it? How was he to turn a grudging invitation to supper into an acceptance of a proposal of marriage? It was not as if he could pretend to be anything other than a fortune-hunter. Leah Falcon was an intelligent woman who would scarcely be brought to believe that he had fallen violently in love with her. If it had been Edith who had control of her own money – Edith who was pretty and eager for affection and for whom Leah seemed to have little affection.

Paul stopped eating and leaned back in his chair, staring thoughtfully up at the ceiling. A plain sister, a pretty sister – pay attention to one and jealousy would flare in the other. It would be a delicate matter to achieve, but he fancied himself equal to the task. And the reward would be high.

Without warning he remembered his grandfather. Old, white-haired, too frail to follow his trade as a printer, he had huddled, wrapped in an old shawl, by the fireplace and watched, without seeming to see, as the other members of the family came and went. The old man had seldom spoke, and the little he ever said had been largely ignored by everybody else, but there had been one occasion when Paul had stood, quivering with anger, informing his parents that he intended to seek his fortune as a writer.

'A writer! Notions above your station! That's what comes of letting you stay on at the Grammar! Might as well reach for the moon!'

His parents, resentful of his ambition, had spat out the phrases at him in a kind of panic, and he had stood there, hating them, hating the squalid room with its cracked plaster and threadbare carpet and fly-blown wallpaper.

The old man's voice had been as thin and dry as the scraping of a little twig across a window-pane.

'Why not reach for the moon, boy?' it had rasped. 'What's wrong with reaching for the moon?'

Paul had left home soon after that and never bothered to go back. He had felt nothing when a chance meeting with a former neighbour years later revealed that his parents and the old man had died. Only in moments of self-doubt did the memory of that long-ago poverty set a dark pit yawning at his feet, and make him determined never to return to his beginnings.

'Reach for the moon,' he uttered aloud. 'What's wrong with reaching for the moon?'

'Were you wanting anything more, sir?' Jake, freed from his customers, popped his round face through the gap in the half-open door.

'No, indeed.' Paul laid down his knife and fork. 'It was an excellent luncheon, but I'm bidden to the supper at Kingsmead tonight and must save some appetite for that.'

'They say Miss Leah keeps a splendid table,' Jake began, and directed a look of most unflattering surprise at his guest. 'To supper at Kingsmead! Would it be Mr Price who asked you? Begging your pardon for mentioning it, sir, but Mr Price is very free and easy in his ways, and not always clear as to what's due to his position.'

'Miss Leah invited me.'

'Miss Leah! Did she indeed?' Again Jake looked in unflattering surprise.

'Seven-thirty for eight.'

Paul rubbed in the slight advantage.

'Then you'll be wanting a hot bath, sir. I'll have the copper heated. And you'll want someone to lay out your dress-suit.'

'If it's not an inconvenience.' Paul mentally congratulated himself on having made the purchase of a dress-suit the previous year. It was not of the best quality cloth, but even so, it had taken most of his savings. However, it was a distinct advantage to be sartorially correct on occasion.

'I'll see to it, sir.'

Jake withdrew, frowning slightly. It was not that he had ever expected to be invited up to Kingsmead himself. And Miss Leah had a perfect right to ask whomsoever she chose to supper. And a man could earn an honest living even as a reporter. But there was something about Mr Paul Simmons that Jake was beginning to dislike. He could not have put his finger on it exactly, but there was a certain shiftiness – reminded him of a potboy he'd employed once and had to dismiss after he'd been caught dipping into the till.

CHAPTER FOUR

'I look a perfect fright!' Edith cried, with no expectation of being believed.

She posed dramatically before the long mirror in the large bedroom she and Beth shared, the last rays of the sun casting their lustre on her creamy skin. Her turquoise gown, cut slightly too low for a modest supper-party was swathed into a generous bustle. Her hair, released from its plaited coils, was drawn up into a knot of ringlets.

Beth, attired in paler blue, with her honey-coloured hair tied back in schoolgirl fashion, obliged with the expected rejoinder.

'You look perfectly beautiful, Edith! All the men will fall in love with you.'

'Pooh! the vicar, the doctor, the solicitor, and old Colonel Whatsisname who goes on and on about the Crimea!'

'And Mr Simmons,' Beth said slyly, and watched faint colour mantle her sister's cheeks.

'Yes. Leah did mention something about his coming. At least it will be a change from the same old faces.'

Edith took up her blue-feather fan and wafted it energetically to and fro, though the room was really quite cool.

In her own apartment Leah was putting the finishing touches to her own costume. At the last moment she had discarded the sedate lavender she had intended to wear for a gown of nutmeg silk, striped in pale orange, and trimmed with coffee lace. Her dark hair was too straight and heavy to curl, but she had coaxed a wave into the sides and wore it in a looser chignon than usual.

Her mind roved over the preparations for the evening, mentally ticking and storing. Candles trimmed and ready for the lighting, table laid, jellies setting in the pantry, wines cooling, fires lit, flowers arranged, cards and dominoes set out for those who wanted them. She would have to keep a close watch on Edith who was apt to flirt with any male under fifty. Beth, provided her tendency to chatter was checked, could be relied upon to behave herself. John and Price were both making ready in their own rooms at the other end of the long gallery.

Leah pressed her lips together considering her brothers. Price was spending altogether too much time in London, and though John could be trusted to hold the younger in check, there was something troubling John that might dilute his attention. Leah had always been closest to John, but since his return home she had sensed in him a faint withdrawal. No doubt he would confide in her later. Meanwhile she had better go down and greet the guests. She allowed herself one last, critical look in the mirror.

Her waist was nipped into fashionable

tininess, and though she lacked Edith's more opulent curves, her breasts were shapely. For no reason at all she imagined Paul Simmons' hands cupping them, and shivered, with what she told herself firmly was disgust.

A couple of hours later, amid the discreet chattering and muted laughter of guests almost at their ease, she leaned back in her chair and allowed herself to relax for a moment. The occasion was going very well. John was a little quieter than usual though he was never very expansive, and Price had helped himself to rather more of the claret than Leah considered suitable in a lad of nineteen, but the atmosphere was pleasant. That the twenty-odd guests should remain slightly awed was, in her opinion, a tribute to the social superiority of the Falcons. And Mr Simmons was conducting himself like a gentleman. She had glanced over in his direction several times and noted that he had twice refused to have his wine-glass refilled.

'Ladies and gentlemen!' She raised her voice slightly, rapping for attention with her folded fan. 'May I crave your indulgence for a moment? It is hardly becoming for a lady to make speeches, but my brothers and sisters and I would like to welcome you and thank you for coming. Yesterday a memorial window was unveiled in the church to the memory of our parents. This evening I am pleased to be able to tell of another, more ambitious memorial that is to be raised to them. This project has been agreed between my brother and myself, and will come as much a surprise to the rest of the family as it does to you.'

She paused, aware that every eye was fixed upon her in lively curiosity.

'It was always my mother's wish,' Leah continued, 'that a school should be built on the foundations of the old manor house. Unfortunately, both she and my father died before this could be implemented. There has long been a need for a school in Marie Regina, and now I am very happy to be able to tell you that a school is to be built. It will be known as the Lady Margred School, and we hope it will be ready for opening in two years.'

She sat down to a polite spattering of applause and a buzz of comment.

'Are you really going to have a school built?' Edith was asking. 'Won't it mean lots of children running around all over the place?'

'The old manor is on the other side of the river,' Leah reminded her. 'We will have fences erected to enclose part of the grounds, and there will be staff to engage, books to order, many things to arrange.'

'I think the idea is a splendid one,' the vicar said, enthusiasm masking his slight chagrin at not having been consulted. 'Marie Regina ought to have its own school. For a village of this antiquity–'

'Quite so.' It was John who interrupted. 'My sister and I have discussed this at some length.'

'The old manor was burned down years ago,' the Colonel said loudly to nobody in particular. 'Just the shell of the house left. Nothing more. Sad to see an old house in that condition. But you'll have to make rules for the children. Can't have them running about, trampling down the grass, picking the flowers. Give them a good whipping, I'd say. This younger generation is–'

'Ladies, shall we leave the gentlemen for fifteen minutes?' Leah pushed back her chair and rose, her skirts rustling. 'No longer than fifteen minutes, if you please. We require your company, gentlemen.'

She might not be a pretty woman, Paul thought, watching her leave the great hall and move into the drawing-room, but she was a lady to her fingertips.

'When my sister says fifteen minutes she means fifteen minutes,' Price said, moving to sit by him. 'Leah's word is law. You mustn't be surprised if she appoints herself as first headmistress of that school she intends to build.'

'The school,' said John repressively, 'will be built out of the resources of the main estate.'

'I certainly don't intend to dip into my own pocket,' Price said airily.

'You say the old manor was burned down,' Paul said. 'Years ago. Originally this estate belonged to two families,' John said. 'The Falcons owned this side of the river and the Fleets the other. Eventually they inter-married and Kingsmead became the family home, but people lived in the manor from time to time. The place was burned down – oh, it must have been in my grandfather's time. Some kitchen maid was careless and let a log smoulder on the carpet. The shell of the building is still there, but it'll be pulled down and a completely new building raised.'

The Colonel launched into a pointless anecdote concerning a house that he had once owned, and under cover of the general bustle as cigars and brandy were offered, Paul wandered away from the table and stood examining the tapestries.

It was impossible to tell what they represented, for their brilliant colours had long since faded into grey, and only the shadowy outline of an occasional face hinted at past design. In many places the heavy cloth was frayed and rubbed. Yet it was of a piece with the rest of the furnishings, with the bare flagstones and heavily carved furniture, the pewter and silver gleaming on the high dresser, the spiked candelabra radiant with light, the stairs leading up to the portrait-hung gallery.

There was a slight movement at his side and Leah spoke, a tinge of disbelieving amusement in her voice.

'You are not interested in old needlework surely?' 'The past interests me,' he said. 'Tradition is very important, I think.'

'We feel alike.' She looked pleased. 'Both John and I have the deepest affection for this house. Edith and Price care nothing for it, and Beth is stuffed full of silly legends. But Kingsmead has been Falcon property for three hundred and fifty years. I am determined to retain it as it always was.'

'I wish you success, Miss Falcon,' he said sincerely. 'I thank you.' She gave a little bow and half-turned, one eyebrow raised in her brother's direction.

'Gentlemen, shall we join the ladies?' John said promptly, draining his glass, and throwing a quelling look towards Price who had remarked audibly,

'By Jove! that was a fast fifteen minutes!'

Obediently they were filing through into the long drawing-room. The French windows were open in tribute to the warmth of the evening, but logs blazed in the wide hearth, and the colours of the furnishings blurred into apricot and rose within the radiance of the firelight.

'Come and sit down,' Leah invited still cordial. 'You have not forgotten that you promised to let me have a copy of your proposed article?'

'I wish you had not reminded me,' Paul said. 'I was beginning to feel as if I were a guest, not a man who is supposed to write an article for a newspaper.'

'You don't enjoy your profession?'

'I told you that it's a way of earning a living,' Paul said. 'My true love has always been literature.'

'Oh, yes, your novel. Is it about the past?'

'It's autobiographical,' he said, with an assumption of shyness. 'Don't all novelists begin by examining their own lives?'

'Perhaps.'

'The writing of a novel,' he said earnestly, 'drains one. The writing of an article is – a trivial matter.'

'Not to those who feature in it,' she said sharply. 'It is no pleasure for us to have our privacy invaded!'

'Which makes me regret that I ever accepted the task. I am very grateful for your hospitality, Miss Falcon, and very conscious of the pride you take in your position.'

'Which is justified!' she flashed.

'And ought not to be exposed to common gaze. Upon my word, Miss Falcon, but you tempt me to forget everything I intended to write about you.'

She stared at him, a small frown puckering her smooth brow.

'Leah! do come and make up a four, there's a dear girl.'

A matronly lady who had been introduced as the doctor's wife loomed up, and Leah smilingly excused herself. She was replaced by Beth who sat down without invitation, tossed back her mane of hair, and said,

'Now, aren't you glad that I made Leah invite you? Isn't it an elegant evening?'

'Very elegant, but isn't it a little dull, with no people of your own age?'

'I don't know any people of my own age,' Beth said cheerfully, 'and I don't expect I'd like them very much if I did.'

'But surely you went to school?'

'We had a governess until I was thirteen,' Beth told him, 'but she was a silly mouse of a woman. She gave in her notice and went off and married a curate. After that Mam gave me my lessons. The boys went away to school of course.'

'And now there's to be a school here.'

'Yes.' Her round face darkened slightly. 'I wish they would leave the old manor house alone. It's only a shell now, like the ghost of a building, but ghosts ought not to be disturbed. Are you going to write about the school in your article?'

'I don't know.'

'Leah thinks it's very demeaning to have your name in a newspaper,' Beth confided, 'but Edith and I think it will be rather exciting. Will you write about the Falcon witches?'

'I'm afraid people don't believe in witches any more.'

'In these parts they do,' she said, 'but the countryfolk have more sense than townsfolk. And witches are not always old and bent. Sometimes they are young.'

'And tell fortunes in crystals?' he enquired teasingly.

'Beth! You're to go and turn the music while Miss Semple performs,' Edith interrupted, drifting up.

'And Miss Semple never knows when she's reached the end of a page,' Beth mourned, making a face as she rose.

A few seconds later the strains of a waltz played as Strauss never intended, filled the room.

'Do let us take a breath of air,' Edith begged, glancing towards the open windows.

'Don't you enjoy music?' Paul enquired.

'I love it,' Edith said, with a small, shuddering glance towards the pianoforte. 'That is why I have a sudden craving for air.'

'Poor Miss Semple!' He rose and followed her out onto the night-scented lawn.

The grass stretched away from them past beds of roses and clumps of laurel to the crowded shapes of trees that obscured the dark sky. Behind them light and laughter and the tinkling piano spilled out into the gloom.

'It's very beautiful here,' Paul said.

'I hate it!' Edith spoke pettishly, walking rapidly into the deeper shadows. 'I detest it, Mr Simmons. There is nothing to do at

Kingsmead, nothing to amuse one, nothing for which to hope!'

'A young lady like yourself,' he objected, 'Surely has every hope.'

'Of marriage?' She gave a bitter little laugh. 'Not if Leah has her way. Kingsmead is my sister's god, and gods need sacrifices. She has made John see it as a god too, but not Price or me. We still have minds of our own.'

'But how could marriage–?'

'Hurt Kingsmead? Because then our money would go to our husbands, and none of it would help the upkeep of the estate. When I have the handling of my own money I'll see that not a penny-piece goes into *that!*'

She jerked her head towards the house.

'But surely it's possible for you to be independent now?' he said.

'By earning my bread as a governess or companion, until I come into my ten thousand a year? If Mam had lived she would have seen me provided with a husband, but Mam died. And Leah was always clever. I was almost engaged once, you know. It was during our London season. I had lots of beaux, and one of them was on the verge of proposing to me. He never did, and it was a long time before I discovered that Leah had told him I was delicate, too delicate to bear children. I found it out because Price overheard two of his friends talking. And I am not delicate, Mr Simmons! I am not!'

'Indeed, no. You are as strong as a horse,' Leah said from behind them. 'You have also drunk a little too much wine, my dear sister. Perhaps you would return to our guests now? Mr Stone is to honour us with a song.'

Edith gave her sister a look whose fury could be measured even in the dimness, and flounced indoors.

'My sister Edith is very foolish sometimes,' Leah said, moving to stand by Paul. 'She talks too freely and often to the wrong people.'

'Am I the wrong person?' he asked boldly.

'Aren't you?' She faced him, her head high, her slim shoulders back. 'You are here to write about our affairs. What you have just heard would make a fancy titbit for the scandal sheets. Your editor would pay you well for such information, I imagine?'

'Probably.'

'And will you write about it?' Her voice was cold, but he sensed anxiety held in check.

'I came here to write about the memorial service,' he said tonelessly. 'But any extra information would be seized upon by a good journalist.'

'Are you a good journalist?' she demanded.

'I am a novelist,' he reminded her.

'So you told me – with your book still unpublished! It will cost money to launch a book by yourself.'

'The publication of an exclusive feature on the private lives of an aristocratic family would be well-paid, as you said yourself. Such remuneration would go a considerable way towards launching a book.'

Leah made an impatient gesture with her hands and spoke tartly,

'Can we be done with fencing, Mr Simmons? How much would you need to publish your book?'

'In return for not revealing that you prevented your sister's engagement?'

'You put the matter very crudely,' she said angrily.

'It is a crude matter, Miss Falcon,' Paul said, 'and you do me an injustice by leaping to such a conclusion. I have not indicated that I am willing to be bribed.'

'If you publish such a tale we will take it to

Court,' she said, low and furious. 'There are laws of libel–'

'Neither have I said that I intend to publish anything.'

'A few words spoken by a jealous girl,' Leah said scornfully.

'Coupled with the past history of the family,' he continued smoothly. 'Is it true that a witch is born into every generation?'

'Superstitious rubbish! Nobody believes such nonsense.' 'They might not believe it, but they would read it avidly.'

'So you do intend to hold us up to ridicule, after all your talk of culture and tradition!'

She began to walk across the lawn, her skirts rustling over the grass, her head bent. From the lighted drawing-room the notes of the piano tinkled out mockingly.

'I meant what I said.' Paul quickened his own steps to keep pace with her. 'I am of good family myself, Miss Falcon, though we fell upon hard times – but I need not bore you with that. I grew up in poverty and I am not ashamed of it, but I was born with talent and ambition, and the desire for something better than what I had. This house is the most beautiful house I've ever seen. It has pride and dignity.'

'How odd,' Leah said, stopping suddenly and gazing at him as if she were trying to read his expression through the darkness, 'that you should feel like that. I have never even heard John express it so.'

'And feeling as I do,' he said, 'it would make no sense if I were to write a cheap piece of sensationalism, not when I am so exceedingly ambitious.'

'For a literary career?'

'For a wife.' He was glad of the darkness, for the idea, starting in its simplicity, had leapt full-blown into his mind. 'I am past thirty, Miss Falcon, and at my age a man begins to think of settling down. Your sister is a very charming young woman.'

'Edith! You would dare to–!'

'Miss Edith is of age, isn't she?'

'But not yet in control of her inheritance!' Leah snapped.

'I know. Money is not my main reason for seeking a wife. But to share common interests, to build together for the future–'

'With *Edith!* My sister hasn't a brain in her head,' Leah said. 'I doubt if she's ever read a book in her life, and she has no love for Kingsmead. She never did have you know.'

'But I could hardly aspire to *your* hand, Miss Falcon.' He allowed a slightly wistful note to creep into his voice. 'It's not likely that you would consider me as a husband, is it? You would think of me as a fortune hunter, and there would be some justice in your thinking so.'

He was afraid for a moment that he had over played his hand and that she would order him to leave, but she stayed silent, her toe circling the grass, her smooth head bent. When she spoke her voice was thoughtful,

'I am not displeased by your frankness, Mr Simmons. Frankness is a rare quality these days. One does not often find it in gentlemen, and I do begin to regard you as a gentleman despite your incredible intentions regarding my sister. Those I am not disposed to take seriously.'

'Miss Edith would not welcome my attentions?'

'Miss Edith would welcome almost any attentions!' Leah exclaimed. 'Ever since she was taken to London she has behaved as if the only goal worth achieving was marriage, no matter who the bridegroom might be. She makes a fool of herself over every man she meets. And she is younger than I am! Do you think that I will sit idly by while my younger sister flaunts it up the aisle with the first male she can lay her hands on?'

The jealousy was laid bare now, ugly as a festering wound.

'I cannot imagine,' Paul said cautiously, 'any gentleman of sensibility overlooking you in favour of your sister. Beauty will fade in time, Miss Falcon.'

'But not beauty of character,' she said quickly. 'Integrity, love of tradition, honesty, faithfulness, those things do not fade.'

'But Miss Edith is of age and free to wed where she pleases?'

'We are both of age,' Leah said flatly. 'We may both wed where we choose. And now, if you will excuse me, I have to return to my guests and bring this extraordinary conversation to an end.'

'You will allow me to call upon you tomorrow morning?'

'I thought you had proposed calling upon my sister,' Leah said tartly.

'I did undertake to show you the draft of my article.' 'Then you are not going to–?'

'I am not going to include anything that might embarrass or distress you,' he said gently.

'I was right,' she said slowly. 'You are, at heart, a gentleman. But I do not approve of you seeking my sister's company. I cannot prevent it, but I do not approve.'

'When one cannot obtain wine,' Paul said, 'one drinks water, Miss Falcon. Would you excuse me if I left now? I intend to walk back to the inn and go over what I've written. Will you say good night to the others and thank you for a very pleasant evening.'

He bowed and walked rapidly away without looking back. Leah went on standing on the lawn, her head bent, her toe still circling. She was shaken in that moment by a variety of conflicting emotions. Jealousy of Edith, fear of public scandal, indignation at the reporter's pretensions – these vied with an excitement that crept through her veins like a fever. To marry a man from the lower classes, to bring out in him the talent that his circumstances made impossible for him to express, to show Edith that she too could be desired. Her heart was beating rapidly and she put up her hand to still it and touched again the unawakened roundness of her breast.

CHAPTER FIVE

'Marry Paul Simmons! You must have completely lost your senses!' Edith cried.

'I have a perfect right to marry whom I choose,' Leah said stiffly.

'But you've not known him above a month. Why, he'd have gone back to London long since, if he hadn't decided to stay on in the village. And he never wrote the article about the memorial service after all!'

'He sent in his resignation to the newspaper,' Leah said. 'He respected my own distaste for publicity.'

'And hung around to make eyes at you,' Edith said.

'His behaviour has been impeccable,' Leah said, spots of colour flaming in her cheeks. 'He has acted like a gentleman.'

'A gentleman! Why, you said yourself that a newspaper reporter could never be a gentleman because of the very nature of his profession.'

'Mr Simmons is a novelist. His work on the newspaper was of a temporary nature only.'

'Until he found a rich wife, or is he pretending to be in love with you for yourself alone?'

'Mr Simmons has been completely honest with me,' Leah said. 'Naturally it will be of the greatest help to him not to have to earn a living while he is struggling to establish himself in the literary world. A man would be a fool not to consider that when he took a wife.'

'And Paul Simmons is no fool!' Edith snapped. 'He is making a fool of you, Leah. Depend upon it, but once he has your money he will give up all thought of novel writing.'

'We will have to wait and see,' Leah said smugly. 'Mr Simmons and I see no point in a long engagement. I am an independent woman–'

'Past your first youth,' Edith put in.

'And Mr Simmons has no family. We will be married very quietly at Christmas, so you may as well make up your mind to it. Beth, be kind enough to remove that irritating smirk from your face. It's exceedingly ill-bred!'

With that parting shot Leah went out, closing the bedroom door softly behind her. The younger girls stared at each other, and then Edith sank down on the bed and burst into noisy tears.

'Leah means to humiliate us all!' she wept. 'She has never shown the slightest inclination to marry, and now she intends to foist a low-born Cockney on us!'

'You thought he was very handsome when he first came,' Beth said. 'You were very pleased when you heard he was coming to supper. I thought you were going to set your cap at him.'

'Set my – what ridiculously old fashioned expressions you use! I have never even considered Mr Simmons as a possible husband,' Edith said crossly, blowing her nose.

'Then you ought not to mind so much about Leah's marrying him,' Beth said.

'I don't mind in the least,' Edith said. 'I am not in the least concerned about Leah's husband. Why, she may wed the sweep for all I care. I am quite indifferent, I assure you.'

And demonstrating her complete indifference Edith flung herself down on the counterpane and burst into a fresh storm of weeping.

Leah, holding herself erect to control her shaking, went downstairs and into the solar at the front of the house. The small, oak-panelled room had always been a refuge for her in times of trouble. She had come here to cry silently on many occasions when she had been younger and had not learned to control her tears. She could see herself, plain and gawky, her hair stiffly plaited, weeping silently for fear anybody should hear. Papa had been playing with Edith who snuggled against him, her blonde curls drooping over his arm. Mam had been nursing Beth who was plump and sweet and just beginning to totter unsteadily from one pair of arms to the next. And Leah had curled up on the window-seat, weeping silently for fear anybody should hear.

But not any longer! She would never again weep by herself because she was not loved as much as her sisters. From now on she would have a husband. That he was not from her own class might cause some talk, but he had assured her that he was of good family and, his relatives being dead, there was no danger of their turning up at the wedding to embarrass her. And he would naturally be very grateful that she had agreed to marry him, so grateful that there was every chance she would be able to mould him as she desired. It would be interesting to launch him upon the literary scene, and the fact that she had never met an author or a publisher in her life failed to deter her.

There was not even any need to change the housekeeping routine. The two rooms over the parlour had been dressing room and bedroom for Leah since her mother's death. Paul Simmons would simply move in with her, and take his meals at the long table in the great hall with everybody else. That he would legally control the ten thousand pounds a year she had inherited caused her not a moment's anxiety, as she fully intended to continue to administer her own fortune.

She had sat down in the window-seat and was gazing through the many-paned window into the quiet courtyard. This was the old part of the house, and the part to which she felt closest in spirit. Her one visit to London had been a nightmare she hoped never to repeat. The crowded, stuffy ballrooms where she sat neglected while Edith whirled past on the arms of a dozen different partners, the jostling crowds in the ill-smelling streets, the endless gossip of the chaperones, all had produced in her a distaste bordering on nausea. To return to the tight security of Kingsmead had been an awakening from nightmare. One advantage of wedding a poor man lay in the fact that she would not have to leave her birthplace and live in a strange house in unfamiliar surroundings.

'Are you sick, Leah?'

It was John, coming into the room, who asked the question with some concern, it being unusual for Leah to sit with idle hands.

'I have told Edith and Beth of my plans to marry,' she said.

'How did they take it?' He came over and sat down next to her.

'Beth is too young to have an opinion. Edith was unpleasant.'

'She wishes to be a bride herself,' John commented.

'Her chance will come,' Leah said, 'but meanwhile it would be more pleasant for us all if she behaved properly. It is surely not my fault if Mr Simmons chose me.'

'You are quite certain, are you?' he ventured.

'Certain of what?'

'That Paul Simmons is the man for you. He's not in our class, Leah. I don't find anybody who has ever heard of his family.'

'I don't think that a Falcon need seek betterment through marriage,' Leah said. 'There are more important things than money and position. He has talent and honesty – are we to despise him for that?'

'No, no. Of course not.' Put in the wrong, John flushed slightly.

'I do hope,' said Leah. 'That you are not going to begin to criticize.'

'No, I do assure you. My dear sister, your judgement has always been excellent in all matters,' John said hastily.

'And you need not fear that my marrying will cause me to neglect my duties,' Leah said. 'No, I shall continue to act as hostess for you until your own wedding. Then it will give me great pleasure to hand over the reins to your bride.'

'I was by the Wittle Farm today,' John said. 'Carmody has let the place go to rack and ruin. I've warned him time and time again that I'd not tolerate it. He's taken no notice so I've dismissed him. He may go and play at being bailiff on somebody else's land.'

'You do realize,' Leah said, ignoring the abrupt change of subject, 'that it is your duty to marry?'

'Time enough,' John muttered.

'You are of age,' Leah reminded him. 'It is your duty to provide a male heir to inherit the title and land. Come, you must have thought about it yourself. You come into contact with many nicely-bred girls when you're in London.'

'I'll stay a bachelor and leave the marrying to Price.' 'Price will marry too, of course,' Leah agreed, 'but you are the elder son. Your children will be the next generation of Falcons growing up in our beautiful home–'

'No, they will not!' he interrupted tensely. 'I will have no children! No heirs!'

'But how can you possibly know such a thing?' Leah exclaimed.

'I know it. That's all.' He shifted his position, away from her.

'John, something is troubling you. I've sensed it ever since you came home,' Leah said. 'I thought it might be Price–'

'Price leads his own life. I never interfere.'

'Are you sick then, John, is there some illness? Are you keeping something back from me?'

'I'm perfectly well. It's my affair, Leah, not yours.'

'I never interfere or meddle in your affairs,' Leah said. 'but you cannot throw out dark hints, and expect me to remain silent. You must speak out.'

'It is not a subject for ladies,' John said miserably.

'For heaven's sake, stop behaving as if I were a sheltered schoolgirl!' said Leah in exasperation. 'You say you do not intend to marry, that you will never have children–'

'I've said I don't want to discuss it.'

'And I insist– John, are you trying to say–?' Leah paused, her eyes shocked and anxious.

'I am – incapable,' John said.

'Of fathering children?'

'Of being a husband,' he said flatly.

'But you've never been married, so how – oh, I see!'

Blushing scarlet Leah put her hand to her mouth and emitted a smothered gasp of embarrassment. Aware of the facts of life, she had never connected them with her brothers. She had not imagined either of them to be entirely without experience but she had never allowed herself to think consciously of such matters.

'You are still a very young man,' she said at last. 'It's possible for a young man to be – well – nervous. And such women as would lend themselves to such practices – you are fastidious, John.'

'I went to see a doctor,' he interrupted. 'I went to a specialist, a top man in his field. He told me that my suspicions were justified. It is unlikely that I will ever make a fitting husband for any woman.'

'But not impossible?'

'Not impossible, no. He spoke of research being done.'

'But how could such a thing happen?' she wondered aloud.

'Inbreeding,' John said. 'He asked a great many questions about the family history.'

'Surely you didn't give him your real name!'

'I called myself Price,' John said wearily. 'But I told him what I could remember of the family relationships. Leah, do you realize that Mam and Papa were cousins, and that their grandparents were also cousins? There has been marrying of cousins over and over in our family. The specialist said that inbreeding weakened the strain.'

'An exceedingly coarse remark,' Leah said. 'We are not cattle!'

'Apparently, in breeding, the same rules apply,' John said, with a gleam of humour.

'I refuse to believe it!' Leah rose and paced a few agitated steps. 'And I forbid you to mention one word of this to anybody.'

'I am not likely to go shouting it about the neighbourhood.'

'You have not told Price?'

'I have told nobody, except you.'

'Then we will keep it to ourselves,' Leah

said briskly. 'Depend upon it there is some mistake. You must put it out of your mind for a while, take a tonic perhaps. Later on we can find another specialist, obtain a second opinion. And you must not worry about it. I know very little about such matters, but I'm certain that worrying about them can't help. And I want nothing to cloud my wedding day. Small, tasteful, and select – that is how I wish it to be. Oh, John, you don't think that Great-Aunt Catrin will want to come, do you?'

'Mam's old aunt in Wales, who brought her up? Is she still alive?'

'She was alive a year ago. She's only in her sixties.'

'But she's never been to Kingsmead in her life. She didn't even come to the funeral.'

'She sent a dreadful mourning-card, all written in Welsh,' Leah remembered. 'And when I was little, Papa used to tease me by pretending that he was going to take me for a holiday up to Great-Aunt Catrin.'

'She's a widow, isn't she?'

'With a daughter, I believe,' Leah nodded. 'I've never seen either of them in my life, and I don't think I could endure it if they turned up at my wedding.'

'Wearing woollen shawls and spouting

94

Bible texts!'

John laughed as he spoke, his attention evidently diverted, but the shadow remained in his eyes.

'It really would be dreadful,' Leah mused. 'I know there is nothing in the least shameful about having been born on a small farm, and one has to admire Mam for leaving the place and coming to live with her English cousins–'

'And marrying one of them.'

'It was a happy marriage,' Leah said quickly. 'You know how much they cared about each other. Mam was never the same after Papa was killed.'

'Happy for them, but not for their descendants,' John's voice was bitter.

'Pooh! specialists are frequently mistaken,' Leah said, choosing scorn as a defence. 'Half the time they make wild guesses. I refuse to allow what you have been told to bother me, and you must do the same. When the time comes for you to wed nature will take her usual course.'

'Are you certain, Leah?'

He was the younger child asking for reassurance from the big sister as he had throughout their childhood, and she answered as she had always done,

'Certain sure.'

Later in the day, dressing for supper, she allowed herself the implications of what John had told her. If it were true that he was unable to father children, then his heirs would not inherit Kingsmead, and, the estate being entailed, it would be Price's son who became the next Lord Falcon.

Leah's dark brows rushed together into a frown. She was fond of Price as she was fond of Edith and Beth, but John had always been her favourite. It had never entered her head that she herself might marry, and when she had contemplated the future she had always seen herself as the devoted aunt, caring for John's children. Of John's wife, whoever she might be, Leah had only the haziest notion. A sweet cipher of a girl, she vaguely supposed, would fit into the existing household without disrupting it. It might even be a good idea if the girl were from a slightly lower class. Then her gratitude at having married into the nobility would effectively cancel out any strivings for independence.

But Price would not fit into Leah's scheme of the future. She suspected that he would choose his own wife and insist upon bringing up his children with the same disregard for tradition that he himself had always displayed.

Leah's sallow face stared back at her from the long glass. Behind the face she could see the reflection of the big bed in which her parents and many Falcons before them had slept. Since Mam's death Leah had lain alone under the embroidered quilts, watching the moonlight trail cold fingers across the panelled walls, waking to the touch of sunlight. She did not believe in ghosts, but something of her mother's swift gaieties and swift despair seemed woven into the fabric of the room. Her mother had loved her, but there had never been that closeness of spirit that had been between Mam and Beth.

'Beth carries the mark,' Mam had said, as if excusing her preference, and she had laughed as she spoke, crying out it was all a lot of nonsense anyway and nobody in his right senses would heed it. But it was Beth to whom she had crooned the songs of her childhood and to whom she had told stories of past Falcons, and Leah, her dark plaits drooping over her sampler or lesson, had called out in silent anguish,

'Look at me, Mam. Talk to me, Mam. I am your daughter too.'

And when Mam died she had left 'Witch's

Dower' to Beth. Leah would never have dreamed of moving from Kingsmead to the small cottage that hid itself near the bank of the river, but to possess it would have meant a very great deal.

'Leah, are you busy?'

The small, plumpish shape of her youngest sister hovered in the outer room.

'I'm almost ready.' Leah smoothed down the basque of her tight-fitting bodice and tucked a stray wisp of hair into place. 'What do you want?'

'It's Edith,' Beth said, coming into the bedroom. 'She says she has a headache and asks to be excused from supper.'

'You mean she is still sulking, don't you?'

'She really does have a headache,' Beth said earnestly.

Leah bit her lip, considering Paul would be coming to supper and it would be embarrassing if Edith were to create a scene. And Edith was quite capable of creating a scene. Leah would never forget her hysterical accusations after she had failed to receive a proposal of marriage from young Stanhope.

'Edith had best remain where she is,' she said at last. 'She can have a tray sent up later if her appetite improves. *You* are not suffering from any ailment, I trust?'

'No. Why should I be?' Beth asked in surprise.

'I thought you might have some objection to my bridegroom as Edith seems to have,' Leah said sarcastically.

'I think it's very pleasant for you to be getting married,' Beth said. 'It only bothers Edith because she isn't going to be a bride.'

'Marriage is not a pleasure trip,' said Leah. 'I consider it is my duty to wed. And Mr Simmons is a very talented gentleman. It will be a very great privilege to nurture such talent. He will take his place in the family with no inconvenience.'

'When I get married,' Beth said, 'I won't marry because of duty. I will marry because I'm in love.'

'Naturally affection has its place in matrimony,' Leah said, 'but one cannot build a complete relationship on it. And you are far too young to be bothering your head about marriage.'

'Oh, it doesn't bother me,' Beth said cheerfully. 'If the worst came to the worst I could be a spinster. Edith would hate to be a spinster, but I wouldn't mind it too much. I think I'd go and live at Witch's Dower. There wouldn't be much room at Kingsmead with your children there, and probably John's and

Edith's and Price's too.'

'You really must not be so indelicate,' Leah said severely.

'But people do have babies,' Beth protested.

'It's not a subject to be dwelt on before marriage,' Leah scolded.

'Well, I may not get married,' Beth reminded her, 'and then I won't have any babies. I will simply live quietly in the cottage until I am a very old lady.'

'But if you don't marry and have children,' Leah pointed out, 'you won't be able to leave one of them the cottage. It's never been part of the main estate.'

'I can leave it to you,' Beth said brightly. 'But you never liked the place very much, did you?'

'That's not true,' Leah said quickly. 'I love every inch of our land. But when Mam was alive it was her place, hers and yours.'

'I'll leave it to you then,' Beth promised. 'But I'll likely get married after all. I'm not clever like you or pretty like Edith, but I'm sure someone will have me. I've always had the feeling that one day I would turn a corner and see him, and we'd know each other right off.'

'You set too much store by your feelings,'

Leah said. 'Gentlemen will consider you're eccentric if you go around talking about your feelings.'

'But I can't help having them,' Beth said. 'They come over me so strongly like the time when–'

'When what?'

'I can't remember properly,' Beth said. A dazed expression had crept into her eyes. 'It was darkness I felt, a coldness. Something to do with Mr Simmons.'

'With Paul Simmons? Beth, that's ridiculous!' Leah said sharply.

'At the Memorial Service,' Beth said slowly. 'I remember the window being unveiled, and before that, a darkness around Mr Simmons. It's all blurred now as if it were a dream.'

'Which it probably was! You go about with half your wits missing most of the time.'

Leah spoke crossly, disliking the tremor of apprehension that swept through her. She believed in none of Beth's superstitious nonsense but there was something in the girl's eyes that frightened her.

'I suppose so.' Beth's eyes cleared, their focus narrowing. 'What were we talking about? Oh, yes, is it all right if Edith–?'

'Doesn't come down to supper. Perfectly

all right.'

'I'll tell her.'

Beth swished out, her tail of honey-coloured hair bouncing against her back. Leah stared after her, the apprehension hardening into fear.

The specialist whom John had consulted had talked of inbreeding. Could inbreeding take other forms besides impotence? There had been Falcons in the past whose behaviour had been wild and undisciplined. It was rumoured that her own grandfather, old Nathan Falcon, had committed suicide. Was it possible that in Beth there was some strain of mental weakness?

If that were true, then she must never be permitted to marry. The excitement of a marital relationship might shock her mind into perpetual dreaming. At all costs Beth must be protected.

Leah took a last, critical look at herself in the mirror. Her hair was glossy, her features regular, her teeth even. Lack of colour was no great drawback. There was something a mite vulgar about rosy-cheeked women. And her figure was good, if a trifle too slender for fashion.

A slow smile curved her lips. She had, after all, much to give thanks for. She had a fiancé, the comforts of a beautiful home, ten thousand pounds a year and the distant prospect of a cottage.

CHAPTER SIX

They had been married for six months, Leah thought with satisfaction, and everything was going very smoothly on the whole. As she had expected Paul's arrival had scarcely raised a ripple on the placid waters of the household. He had not attempted to interfere in the running of the estate, indeed he showed no interest in it at all, which was a pity, for John would have appreciated a little help from time to time. But a writer could not be expected to take pleasure in hops and wheat. Not that Paul's book had yet been published. She would have been very willing to defray the cost, but he had decided to rewrite it. She had fitted up the room leading from their bedroom as a study for him, and he spent part of every day there. It pleased her as she went about her household duties to know that he sat there, bent over the handsome desk that had been her father's, the quill pen moving slowly across the heavy vellum. She wished he would show her the results, but he always locked the papers away in the drawer and she had not found where he kept the key.

When he was not writing he sat reading or went for long walks through the fields. She would have enjoyed going with him, but the school rising on the old foundations of the old manor house took up most of her free time.

It was to be a handsome building, designed on classical lines, with large windows to let in the light. There would be two big classrooms, a kitchen where a midday meal could be provided for the children, a parlour where visitors could be shown, and an apartment over it where the teachers could live. Two respectable maiden ladies would be very glad of such a position. There would be furniture to buy, books and slates to provide. She looked upon the whole project as her own personal scheme, and had set aside three thousand pounds a year out of her allowance to pay for the building and running costs. That her money was now legally her husband's scarcely entered her thoughts. When Paul needed money he had only to ask, and being anxious to please him, she saw that his wardrobe was replenished before he noticed that he lacked anything.

Edith was also behaving very well, apart from an occasional fit of temper. She spent most of her time dressing up in one gown after another, or reading yellow-backed novels, but her craving to go to London seemed to have deserted her.

Indeed they were all home again at this period. John seldom went to the city these days, and Price had arrived home six weeks before, announcing that he was giving up his apartment there. He had seemed nervous and ill-at-ease but he had volunteered no information. Leah hoped he might begin to take an interest in the land, but he preferred idling about the village or riding over to Maidstone.

The morning mail had been brought in on the silver salver. Leah set aside the weekly newspaper through which she had glanced, and poured herself a cup of tea. The brew steaming and fragrant, had been brought in with the mail, and she had the solar to herself.

She flicked through the letters with the neat economy of movement that characterized all her actions. Two requests for subscriptions from missionary societies, a bill from John's tailor, a letter from her old governess announcing that lady's impending retirement, a letter for Price.

Leah put down the other letters and raised it to her nostrils. Cheap paper, a scent of violets, a feminine hand slanting backwards as if the writer had been labouring under some strong emotion – her mind registered the facts.

After a moment she lifted the cosy and lid from the teapot and held the letter over the steam, watching the cheap gum begin to dry, the flap to separate.

The letter, headed by a Bayswater address, was very short,

Dear Price,

I know as how I promised not to trouble you but to part friends, only I never knew then as how I was in the family way. The money you gave me will only pay the rent here for three months, and at the end of that I'll not find another gentleman to fancy me.

Hoping you can oblige me,
I remain,
Your devoted servant,
Grace Finn

Leah read the short missive through twice and then refolded the letter carefully, her face blank, her hands steady.

That she had behaved dishonourably in opening the letter never entered her mind. Had she been challenged she would have said it was her duty to take an interest in family affairs.

So Price had seduced a girl and broken off the relationship, before knowing the girl was with child. Leah unfolded the letter and read it a third time. Cheap, scented paper, immature writing with much to be desired in the grammar, but it was correctly spelt and its tone was simple and respectful, carrying no flavour of blackmail. If the letter were not answered the girl might write again, but she was more likely to take herself off to some back-street abortionist. And a child that would have grown up to be a Falcon, albeit on the wrong side of the blanket, would end life before it had begun.

If Leah were to hand the letter to Price he might believe it his duty to make an honest woman of the girl. Nineteen year olds were apt to behave with foolish chivalry; and in that case the future heir of Kingsmead would be the child of Price and a girl called Grace Finn. Leah's mouth thinned to a narrow line, and something cold and ruthless gleamed at the back of her eyes. It was not that she had no affection for Price, but he was not the elder and deep down she considered it unlikely that he would allow her to bring up his children in the manner she considered right. And John, if his belief was true, would never father a child.

After a space she rose, took careful note of the address at the top of the letter, and then thrust it deep into the glowing heart of the fire. Then she poured herself another cup of tea and drank it with relish. There were times when she was pleased that a strong hand guided the family, and even more pleased that the strong hand should be hers.

After the midday meal she intercepted Price as he made his way towards the stables where he intended to check his new hunter.

'Can't whatever you want wait?' he enquired, a trace of impatience in his voice.

'I'd like to speak to you now, in the study,' she said, and went briskly back upstairs.

Paul, having locked away his papers, was stretched at ease in his armchair reading a novel. As Leah came in he looked up, his face tightening unconsciously.

'Is anything wrong, my dear?' There was he reflected, usually something wrong when

Leah came into a room. In the six months of their marriage he had ceased hoping that a passionate and docile woman would emerge from the cool façade of the gentlewoman.

'I wish to talk to Price. It's family business,' she said, with no intention to wound.

'I was just going out.' There was a note of relief in his voice as if he feared that he might be expected to involve himself in the affairs of her relatives.

'I'll see you later then.' She offered a smooth cheek and sat down in the chair he had just vacated, her back erect, her narrow hands folded in the lap of her blue gown.

As he went out he passed Price who raised his eyebrows in question and shrugged slightly, as if there were a bond between them.

'Sit down, Price.'

Leah's voice reminded him of the rare occasions when his father had scolded him for some boyish misdemeanour. It held the same thread of steel. But his involved and picturesque excuses on those previous occasions had softened the steel into silk, reducing his father to laughter. He doubted if Leah had the saving grace of humour.

'Was it so terribly urgent?' he enquired jauntily, flinging himself into the chair she had indicated.

'Price, I have never interfered in your pursuits,' Leah began, in a voice that suggested she was about to start.

'No, indeed. Always appreciated it,' Price said heartily.

'But you are still a month short of twenty,' Leah continued as if he had not spoken, 'and that is not so very old. And it's very obvious to me that you are troubled about something. It has been obvious since you came home.'

Price's face had reddened with chagrin. Trust Leah to ferret out that something was wrong. She had always been the smartest in the family.

'You had better tell me,' Leah said calmly. 'Of course you might prefer to talk to John, but he has a great deal on his mind with the estate to run and his duties in the House–'

'John wouldn't understand. He never wastes a penny,' Price said quickly.

'It's money then.' She kept the surprise out of her voice, having believed him troubled about the girl.

'A fellow has to amuse himself in some way,' Price said with a hint of sulkiness. 'I had bad luck at the tables.'

'You're under age. They should not have

110

allowed you to take part.'

'They don't enquire too closely,' Price said. 'And I would have won if I'd stayed for long enough on the black.'

'Was it just roulette?' she asked.

'Horses too,' he said unwillingly. 'God damn it, but a Falcon ought to be a good judge of horseflesh. It's my belief half the races are rigged. I'll swear the last handicap–'

'How much?' Leah interrupted. 'How much money do you owe?'

Price took a deep, quivering breath, clenched his fists and said,

'Thirty thousand.'

'Thirty thousand *pounds?* Price, until you come of age, your allowance is only two thousand a year! Where did you find the money with which to bet?'

'There are people who are willing to put up your stake,' Price said. 'You're supposed to pay them back when you win, but if you have a run of bad luck they'll wait, for a consideration, of course.'

'Loan sharks,' Leah said tightly. 'I've heard of such men. They specialize in younger sons and charge high rates of interest. Oh, Price, how could you be such a *fool!*'

'You don't know how bored a fellow gets,' Price began, the sulkiness returning to his

face. 'I tried to cut down. I even gave up –
but it's not important now.'

'Gave up what?'

'I was paying the rent of a flat in
Bayswater,' he said reluctantly. 'A neat little
stunner she was too! I was quite fond of her,
but I packed it in.'

'Are you telling me that these people
won't wait any longer for their money?'
Leah demanded.

'They've been dunning me for weeks,'
Price confessed. 'Now I've got until the end
of next month before they get really nasty.'

'You mean they'll come to Kingsmead?
Come here?'

She stared at him in horror, the spectre of
scandal dancing before her eyes.

'There is no limit to what they might do,'
he said, finding a perverse pleasure in his
own gloom.

'Then they must be paid.' She spoke
serenely, but her eyes were hard, her mind
seizing opportunities.

'How? You know the terms of Papa's Will.
I get an allowance from the interest until I
come of age, but the principal remains
untouched until then, and I can't use all of
it then. It's doled out to me annually as if I
were a female!'

'You have less sense than any woman,' Leah said. 'Papa knew there was a reckless streak in your nature even then. It's fortunate for you that John can use his own share as he chooses.'

'John puts it all into the estate.'

'But he would raise the thirty thousand for you if I asked him,' Leah said.

'Would you? Would you do that, Leah?'

Price leaned forward, a coaxing eagerness in his face.

'It would be a loan,' she warned. 'In return he'd expect it in writing that you would give him your first three years' allowance. He'd be justified in charging interest, but I think I can persuade him otherwise.'

'Leah, you're an angel!' Price exclaimed, but she held up her hand.

'I'm very happy to be able to help you, or rather to persuade John to help you,' she said coolly, 'but you need not imagine that I intend to make a habit of it. You will have to set your mind to earning a living for the next few years until your debt has been discharged.'

'Earn a living!' He looked at her in almost comical dismay. 'What sort of living could I make? You'd not expect me to hang about at Kingsmead, watching the crops grow? I could breed horses, I suppose. There's money in bloodstock–'

'I was thinking of the Colonies,' Leah interposed.

'You've always said you'd like to travel. There are opportunities for healthy young men – why, I was reading in the paper only this morning that there are diamonds simply lying around in the Transvaal.'

'In South Africa? There's trouble with the Boers there.'

'Canada then, if you're afraid of a little trouble.'

'I never said that,' Price said quickly. 'It might be exciting. We've hardly been a warlike lot in our family.'

'A Falcon died at Trafalgar,' Leah said.

'And that was nearly a hundred years ago!' Price said scornfully. 'Not that I've any taste for dying in battle! Diamonds, now, are quite a different matter. I could come back as a millionaire in two or three years time!'

'You couldn't go out there penniless,' Leah said, 'but I'd be willing to – stake you? I could let you have a thousand out of my own money. That would pay your passage and give you a start.'

'I wish I'd talked to you before,' Price said. 'You've been very generous, Leah. To tell you the truth, I've been at my wits' end these past weeks. Are you sure that John will agree?'

'You must expect a lecture,' Leah warned. 'However, I don't hold John entirely guiltless. It was his duty to look after you to a certain extent when you were both in London, and he failed in that. But it might be a good idea if you were to arrange to travel very soon. There are crowds of young men heading for the diamond fields, or so the newspaper says.'

'How soon could I book a passage?' he asked.

One of his sudden and usually short-lived enthusiasms had come over him. He would, had it been possible, have packed his bags at once.

'By the end of the month,' Leah said kindly, 'we ought to be able to settle your affairs. But you must think about it for a while. There is no sense in rushing into things.'

'I want to go as soon as possible,' he said, as she had expected he would. 'I want to prove to you that I can make something of myself. I'll come back a rich man, Leah, and give you a diamond necklace. You see if I don't!'

'I'll talk to John this evening,' she

promised. 'You had best leave it to me. Oh, but we must have a full list of your debts and of the men to whom you owe money, and then there will be no danger of anybody turning up in Marie Regina.'

'You're a good sort, Leah,' he said, and gave her a clumsy hug. For an instant she held him tightly, remembering that he was a Falcon and she was sending him away. Then she drew back, smoothing down her dress, and said lightly.

'You'd best sweeten John by offering him that new hunter of yours. I don't expect you've paid for it yet anyway.'

Price, running down the staircase, had a feeling of release as if some prison had opened. It was to be expected that he would miss the family for a while, but he would soon get settled. Diamonds were a good investment, and his luck was due to change. He might find an enormous stone big enough to discharge his debts, and provide all his sisters with diamond necklaces.

Leah, alone in the study, drew several deep breaths and allowed herself to relax slightly. Price she thought, was a young fool, with something weak inherent in him. There had been a seventeenth century Falcon with the same careless charm, the same tendency

116

to gamble. Price reminded her of him.

And he was to become a father! She smiled a little grimly, wondering what his reaction would have been had she told him about it. She suspected he would have married the girl and taken her to South Africa with him. The child destined to be the heir of Kingsmead would have grown up under alien skies.

Her smile widened and became triumphant. A faint colour stole into her cheeks so that, for a moment, she looked almost pretty. Then her eyes fell upon the locked desk and her frown returned. It was hurtful not being allowed to help the husband whose talents she planned to direct and nurture.

It would have pleased her to have sat by his side, listening as he read out what he had written, advising him as to the best way in which to frame a sentence or give life to a character. But Paul had never asked for any help, had never even offered to show her any of his work.

The building of the school and the duties of the household took up a great deal of her time, but she was determined that when the evenings began to draw in she would devote more attention to her husband's pursuits.

Then they would draw even closer together and find in mental companionship the kind of satisfaction she had hoped to find in the physical aspects of marriage.

For the first time the thought that all was not perfect in her life crossed her mind. It was not, she knew, ladylike to admit it, but she had yearned for the satisfactions of physical desire, and the brief moments in the dark that passed between them left her feeling empty, with something inside her still crying out.

She gave a small, unconsciously pathetic, sigh and went out to the broad gallery with its long line of framed portraits. All the masters of Kingsmead and their wives were here, clothed in the garments of their period.

Leah paused, thinking about them more deeply than she had ever thought of them before. For more than three hundred years her ancestors had lived in Kingsmead, beginning as gentlemen squires on con-fiscated monastic land, adding to the property through marriage, squandering or hoarding their wealth, being laid to rest in the churchyard of Marie Regina.

In the painted faces she could see the features of her own brothers and sisters dimly shadowed forth. John had the same patient expression as Grandfather Nathan, and a set of the lips that was like that of Sir Robin Falcon who had supported the Parliament side in the Civil War. It was rumoured that Robin had sired no child but had accepted as his own the daughter that his twin brother had begotten upon his wife. The Cavalier brother, curls touching his wide shoulders, looked at her with Price's eyes.

She could trace Edith's delicate features in the blonde prettiness of Marie Fleet, the cousin from the manor house who had wed the Cavalier brother, and had to bear the humiliation of watching her sister-in-law bear his child.

And that face that stared out of its canvas with a listening look reminded Leah of Beth, though the girl in the picture had drowned as a witch centuries before.

'Too much inbreeding,' Leah muttered.

The specialist had probably been right. The family would grow weaker, might even die out unless practical steps were taken. Well, she had begun aright by taking an outsider as a husband. If she were ever blessed with a child it would be strong and healthy.

John was her chief concern. He was master

of Kingsmead, and she loved him more than the others. John must not be allowed to go through life believing himself to be less than a man.

Her jaw hardened slightly and the cold glitter came back into her eyes. At that moment she looked uncannily like Sir Charles Falcon who had terrorized the family early in the eighteenth century.

Beth, coming up the broad stone stairs, spoke cheerfully,

'If I were standing idle like that, you'd soon be finding me something to do.'

'I was just thinking that these pictures could do with cleaning,' Leah said, not turning. 'The frames would stand regilding too. When I go to London I'll make some enquiries.'

'Are you going to London?' Beth asked with interest, 'What are you going there for?'

'Price has taken it into his head to hunt diamonds in South Africa,' Leah told her. 'He's set on the idea, and I see no point in opposing him, but at least I can ensure he has a comfortable passage.'

'But don't you mind his going?' Beth asked in surprise.

'Naturally we shall all miss him very

much,' Leah said, 'but he is a young man and young men seek adventure.'

'John doesn't.'

'John's duty is to the estate,' Leah said, 'as ours is to John. Price being a young man, has his own life to lead.'

'I thought a wife's duty was to her husband,' Beth said, with a touch of impertinence.

'Yes. Yes, it is,' Leah said absently, 'but families count for a very great deal.'

'And wishing,' said Beth.

'Wishing for what?' Leah enquired.

'For all the things you want,' Beth said. 'Don't you ever wish on the new moon, Leah?'

'I have better ways in which to occupy my time,' Leah said, 'and so should you have. Wishing on the moon indeed!'

CHAPTER SEVEN

Grace kicked off her shoes, watched indifferently as one of them landed in the centre of the plush covered table, and reclined as comfortably as her corsets would permit on the chaise-longue.

She had been very proud of her small apartment when Price Falcon had installed her in it eighteen months before. It was only sitting-room and bedroom with a slip of a kitchen and a tiny bathroom, but she had her own front door, a handsome, good-natured lover, a steady engagement in the chorus of a successful musical comedy, and the kind of looks that made other women raise their eyebrows.

The Irish blood of her grandparents was apparent in her smoky blue eyes and faintly freckled white skin. Her hair was an inheritance too, being of that brilliant Titian that frequently looks dyed when it isn't. It was swept up into a cascade of tiny ringlets ornamented with little glittering rhinestones, and her dress was of that slightly over elaborate style which proclaimed her as a member of the theatrical profession.

It was seldom that Grace reviewed the twenty years of her life, for she was not by nature, analytical, but on this warm June afternoon, she was so depressed by the turn of recent events that she began to wonder how matters could have come to such a pass. It was not as if she were either ignorant or inexperienced. A girl who had been brought up in the back streets of the East End had to be tough in order to survive, and Grace had learned at an early age how to take care of herself. She had been more fortunate than most in that her parents had scraped together sufficient to provide her with a meagre education. They had hoped to place her in service in one of the big houses up west, but Grace's striking looks had been noticed by a gentleman engaged in forming a troupe of juvenile dancers, and at fourteen she had found herself bound for the provinces with eleven other young hopefuls.

The life had been hard and devoid of glamour, but she had enjoyed the constant travelling, the changes of scene, the applause of the audience after the long hours of rehearsal. She had also had the good sense to realize that she possessed very little dramatic talent. She could dance adequately and her singing voice was pretty, but her main appeal lay in her excellent figure, her vivid hair, and her lively personality. At sixteen she had returned home to bury her parents, both victims of an influenza epidemic, and had resumed her career as a solo dancer, the troupe having disbanded for lack of funds. Many girls in her position would have escaped into matrimony or sunk into the twilight existence of the street walker.

Grace secured a steady string of chorus engagements, sometimes in the provinces, occasionally in the West End. She had a reputation for hard work and good-humour, was on pleasant but not intimate terms with other members of the company, and took the occasional lover merely as an economic necessity between jobs.

Price Falcon had been scarcely more than a schoolboy, but she had enjoyed his body, accepted his offer of an apartment, and drifted into what seemed like a permanent arrangement. The revelation of his financial difficulties had been a shock, but being far too sensible to argue she had parted from him amiably, aware that she had three months in which to find fresh accommodation.

The discovery that she was pregnant had been a severe blow. Even with tight lacing she could not continue to appear on stage for longer than four or five months, and she had never saved any of her salary.

The prospect of aborting the child had been dismissed, not on moral grounds, but because Grace had the distaste of a normal, healthy young woman for the trade carried on, in filthy conditions, by women of dubious reputation. Moreover, enjoying life as she did, she was reluctant to deprive her own flesh and blood of it.

Her letter to Price had been written with every expectation of its being answered. She was certain that he would contrive to send her sufficient to tide her over until after the child's birth. Then she could foster it with some respectable woman and take up her career again.

It had all seemed very simple but nearly three weeks had elapsed since the sending of the letter, and no word had come. She was also feeling less than energetic for each day began with a prolonged bout of nausea that left her feeling weak and dizzy, and she already seemed to be putting on weight.

The room was too stuffy. She thought how pleasant it would be to walk out into green fields where the air was sweet. Once, when she had been a member of the troupe, they had all gone into the country for a picnic. She had never forgotten the scratchiness of the long grass against her legs, the scent of clover, the fat, lazy cows.

The doorbell chimed twice before she realized that anybody was there. She was across the room and in the tiny hallway quickly, her mind filled with the sudden hope that Price had come to see her.

A strange woman stood on the threshold, her dark mulberry skirts and cream-veiled toque displaying the understated elegance of a lady. She was, Grace judged, in her mid-twenties and devoid of beauty though she had fine eyes.

'Miss Finn?' Her voice was clear and well modulated.

'Yes?'

'You are Miss Grace Finn?'

'Yes, ma'am.'

'My name is Simmons. Leah Simmons. May I come in for a few moments as I have some private business to discuss with you?'

The tone was polite, the manner gentle, but Grace had admitted her visitor and ushered her to the most comfortable chair before she realized it. She was aware, as she did so, that the other had cast a swift, raking glance about the room, a glance that registered every detail from the coffee-stain on the cushion to the shoe on the table. Hastily, Grace retrieved both her shoes and, feeling at a distinct disadvantage, sat down again on the chaise-longue.

'Would you like some tea?' she asked nervously, feeling personally that this was one of the rare occasions when she would have welcomed a nip of something stronger.

'Thank you, but no. It is not long since I had luncheon.'

'Then what can I do for you? You mentioned business, but I'm sure we never met before.'

'I am Price Falcon's sister,' said the lady.

'Oh,' said Grace blankly. Then the colour surged up into her face and she said again. 'Oh. I see.'

'It will save us both a great deal of time,' Leah said coolly, 'if I tell you at once that I am aware of your association with my brother. I am also aware that you are expecting his child. You are certain that it is his child?'

'I don't know what you're hinting at,' Grace said, her natural spirit returning, 'but I've not had a gentleman friend since I took up with Price, and that's more than a year ago. Not that I saw him except when he was in town, but I kept myself respectable meantime.'

'You work, I take it?'

'Yes, ma'am. I'm an actress, musical comedy. Small parts mainly, but I pay my own way.'

'My brother installed you here.'

'And all he ever paid was the rent,' Grace said. 'I took a small present now and then, flowers and a fan and a nice brooch, but I've been in regular work since I took up with Price.'

'Which will cease as your pregnancy advances. You wrote to Price.'

'Not to cause him any trouble,' Grace said quickly. 'I was fond of Price for all he's younger than me and not very clever at managing his money, and I didn't want to make trouble, but it's his child and he's a right to know.'

Leah studied her face thoughtfully. The girl's sincerity and lack of malice impressed her. Certainly she was not a lady, but she was handsome and intelligent with none of the little affectations of speech or manner that another in her position might have been tempted to assume.

'Can you tell me something of your family?' Leah enquired.

'Why, there was only my parents and they died four years back,' Grace said. 'Took the influenza and died in the same week. I'd been on the boards, the stage that is, for a couple of years before that. I was a Juvenile.'

'You have no other family?'

'No, ma'am. They only ever had the one

child, though Dad used to say it wasn't for the want of trying.'

Leah, wincing slightly at the crudity, said, 'What did you hope for from my brother? Financial support? He is not yet in possession of his full inheritance. And he was being dunned.'

Grace nodded in agreement. 'That's why we had to split up. But I did hope, that when he heard about the child, he'd come up with a bit of the ready.'

Leah again suppressed a shudder. The girl certainly used some coarse expressions.

'My brother sailed for South Africa this morning,' she said. 'I came to London to bid him farewell.'

'I see.' Grace stared at her ringless fingers and gave a little, resigned sigh. 'So that's that.'

'Not quite. There is the child.'

'It's your brother's child,' Grace said defensively.

'I have no doubt of it,' Leah said. 'You must be feeling very much alone, my dear.'

Her voice was unexpectedly gentle and there was sympathy in her face.

'I'm at my wit's end,' Grace said. 'I can't keep on dancing much longer, that's sure; and I've not been well at all.'

'But you come of healthy stock?' Leah interrupted. 'No record of lung or heart disease in your family?'

'No. I've never had a day's illness,' Grace said in bewilderment.

'And naturally you wish for some provision to be made for you.'

'I'd no wish to cause any trouble,' Grace said.

'Were you fond of my brother?' Leah asked. 'You didn't seem very disturbed when I told you that Price had left the country.'

'It's no good crying over spilt milk,' Grace said, with an air of originality. 'Price and I rubbed along very well, and I thought a lot of him, but he was never that serious about me.'

'There was never any question of – marriage?' Leah laced her finger-tips together and waited for the reply.

'Bless your heart, no,' Grace said. 'Young gentlemen in Price's position don't marry girls like me!'

'Grace – may I call you Grace? – I have a proposition to put to you,' Leah said slowly.

'A proposition?' Grace looked puzzled.

'You do intend to have this child I take it?' Leah questioned sharply.

'Yes, I do. Not that it's any joke, ma'am, to bear a child out of wedlock,' Grace said earnestly, 'but I do believe it has a right to be born.'

'Would you like it to be born in wedlock?' Leah asked. 'But you said Price had—'

'Not Price. His brother, John.'

'John?'

'Surely you have heard of Price's elder brother, Lord Falcon?'

'Yes, Price never said very much about his family, but he did tell me he had a brother. Quiet and sat in the House of Lords or some such place.'

'John is willing to marry you,' Leah said.

'Willing to – but he doesn't know me. We've never met!'

'It is the custom, I believe, in China for gentlemen to wed ladies they've never seen.'

'That's all very well,' Grace said, recovering her poise a little, 'but we don't live in China.'

'Nevertheless John is willing to marry you.'

'After I've been with Price!'

'John is not, and never will be, aware of that,' said Leah. 'He is not, at this moment, even aware of your existence.'

'I don't understand,' Grace said flatly. She began to wonder if Leah were a little mad.

'My brother, John, is shy and quiet,' Leah said patiently. 'He is also greatly occupied by his duties on the estate. He wishes to marry. Indeed his position would seem to demand that he take a wife, and in this matter he is willing to be guided by me.'

'Only trust me, John,' she had urged. 'and I will find you a charming girl who will quickly prove the specialist was wrong.'

'You mean he'll let you choose a wife for him!' Grace exclaimed in disbelief. 'But what happens when he finds out that I'm carrying his brother's child?'

'There is very little likelihood of his ever finding out,' Leah said tranquilly. 'Price did not, I hope, advertise his liaison with you?'

'He never told anyone. He said his family might disapprove,' Grace said.

'And South Africa is such a long way away and Price so lazy about writing letters.'

'But I don't understand,' Grace said helplessly. 'Why would you want me to marry your brother at all? I'm not in your class. I know that.'

'A great deal of nonsense is talked about class, don't you think?' Leah said smoothly. 'My own husband is not from what might be termed the gentry, but he is a most talented writer. And you seem to me to be a most admirable young woman. John will be very happy with you, and I'm certain you will find nothing to complain of in his conduct towards you.'

'It's not me, is it?' Grace said. 'It's the child. I think you want the child. Well, I'm willing for it to be reared by you. I'm not the maternal type.'

'The child must be born in wedlock,' Leah said. 'These are not olden times when such things were tolerated. There have been too many scandals in high society recently, a definite decline in moral standards.'

'So I am to marry your brother and pretend the child is his? That doesn't sound very moral to me,' Grace said forthrightly.

'Let me put it another way,' Leah said. 'In return for keeping silent about the true father of your baby you will acquire a luxurious home, an affectionate husband, and a title. You will no longer be Grace Finn of the musical comedy stage. You will be Lady Grace Falcon of Kingsmead.'

'Lady Grace Falcon.' The girl tasted the syllables on her tongue.

'Price is not likely to come home claiming the child as his own,' Leah said. 'It was his decision, after all, to go to South Africa.'

'I must have time to think,' Grace said

distractedly. 'How do I know you mean all this? How do I know that you're who you say you are?'

'My marriage lines are in my reticule if you insist on seeing them,' Leah said coldly. 'But you can't pretend to disbelieve me.'

Grace got up and took several turns about the room. It was incredible, the most incredible happening in her life, but she had no reason to suppose it was not true. Leah Falcon or Simmons or whatever her name was had actually made the unbelievable offer, and she Grace Finn, was about to become Lady Falcon, if she chose.

'I can give you until tomorrow morning,' Leah said, rising in her turn. 'I am staying at my brother's apartments tonight. The others were not able to come and say goodbye to Price. They have their duties at home to attend, and I cannot afford any more time away myself. I will come back tomorrow morning, and if you are willing to accept what, in my opinion, is a very generous arrangement, we can travel to Kingsmead together.'

'It seems like selling myself,' Grace said uneasily.

'For the sake of the child,' Leah said gently. 'Would you not put aside your scruples for the sake of the child? If you decide sensibly you will have to give in your notice at the theatre, I suppose? I trust there will be no difficulties. No I'll see myself out, thank you. I am sure you will be very happy with us, my dear. We are a very close and loving family. Price's absence will be felt by all of us, but one cannot hold back a young man from seeking adventure.'

She shook hands cordially and was gone, the faintest scent of her lavender cologne lingering in the room.

Grace, standing by the window, watched her step up into a waiting cab. There was breeding on every line of the slim figure, and a ruthlessness in the set of the narrow shoulders. For no reason she could fully understand, Grace shivered. There was a darkness in the room though the sun was still shining, and her hands were cold.

She went over to the fireplace and, kneeling to warm herself, tried to remember what Price had told her about his home. It had not been very much. Indeed he had given the impression that he cared very little for the place and certainly did not begrudge the fact that his elder brother had inherited both title and estate. He had referred to John as a quiet sort with whom he seemed to have little in common, and he had hardly mentioned his sisters at all, apart from one called Edith, of whom it appeared he was rather fond.

Their relationship, Grace admitted to herself, had been based on a wholehearted enjoyment of each other's bodies. She had been an undemanding mistress and their meetings had been discreet. Price, when he came to town, visited her during the day, although he occasionally came to see the show and escorted her home afterwards.

With a brief spasm of irritation, Grace thought it was typical of his casual attitude to sail off to South Africa when he had learned of her condition and leave others to clear up the resulting mess. It would serve him right if she did marry his brother and he came home to find her installed as lady of the manor. But what sort of man allowed his sister to choose a bride for him? An innocent, she supposed, who could be deceived into think that another man's child was his own. 'Gentle, kind and quiet, but a bit of a prude' were the words Price had used of him. Probably undersexed, Grace had decided, and wondered if that would trouble her very much.

But it was a risk, a challenge. She had

taken a risk six years before when she had talked her parents into allowing her to join the theatrical troupe, and that hadn't paid off too badly. Perhaps it was time to take another risk. The alternative was a bastard child and, for girls like her, that was often the first step towards prostitution.

And at the back of her mind was the memory of that picnic in the country, when they had all sat in a meadow, and drunk lemonade, and picked great bunches of blue and yellow flowers, and piled back into the omnibus for the drive back to the theatre just as the sun was setting and the pale disc of the moon rising. It had been the first time she had noticed sun and moon in the sky at the same time, and they had both looked near enough to touch.

A big house in the country would be a marvellous place in which to bring up a child; and there was no denying it would be marvellous to be Lady Falcon. Chin on hand, Grace brooded into the little, leaping flames on the hearth.

Leah, having entered the cab, sat erect on the leather seat and stared through the window as the vehicle lumbered through the crowded streets. Banners and flags expressing loyal greetings, hung limply, remnants of the Queen's Jubilee celebrations, and there were an unusual number of visitors who had stayed on to see the sights of the capital.

Her eyes took in little of the passing scene. She detested London and found no pleasure in tall buildings and noisy crowds. Her visit on this occasion, however, had been, she considered, a success. Indeed she had planned it as carefully as any general planning a campaign.

Price, immersed in preparations for his voyage, had certainly not noticed the long, confidential talks between Leah and John.

'We cannot stop Price from doing what he wants to do,' Leah had said. 'But his going means that you must marry. Believe me, but the longer you wait the more difficult it will be.'

John, worried by the sudden demand on his capital for the purpose of lending Price sufficient to discharge his debts, had listened with a weary, resigned look on his face and agreed. Leah, he thought, would probably arrange everything very nicely as she usually did. She had been over to Maidstone to see the family solicitors with a view to sorting out Price's financial affairs; had booked a passage to South Africa for her brother and provided him with tropical

138

kit, and would probably return from London with a suitable bride in tow.

'No need to mention our little scheme to Price,' Leah had said. 'It is not after all as if you had taken him into your confidence. When the young lady arrives, I think we will let Edith and Beth assume that you have known each other for some time. That will be best.'

It probably would be best. Leah, thought John affectionately, was always right. And the young lady, whoever she might be, would be eminently suitable. In the midst of his affectionate musings John found himself sighing, an intolerable weight upon his spirits. Perversely he could almost wish that Leah was occasionally wrong.

Leah was thinking about Grace Finn. A healthy, good-humoured young woman like that would make a splendid wife and mother. She dressed badly, of course, and her education had been neglected, but she seemed intelligent, and she was certainly shrewd enough to realize the advantages that Leah was offering. If John were truly impotent the girl would not dare to complain for fear of compromising herself, and yet if she were as experienced as Leah suspected she would contrive to make John believe he was the father of the child.

All in all everything was working out in a very satisfactory manner. In a year or two when John and Grace had settled down to married life, when the babe had safely arrived, when the school had been built and Paul's novel published, then Edith would have to be considered. The silly girl would never be contented until she was wed, and it was not to be expected that she would ever have the sense to choose a suitable mate.

And then there was Beth. It would never do to allow Beth to marry, to allow the queerness that was in her to develop. Beth would have to be protected.

They had reached the quiet street where John's town apartments were situated. As she paid off the driver and alighted from the cab, a sense of all her responsibilities flooded through her. It was an unfortunate fact that of the five children born of the ideal love-match between her parents, only she had any strength of will or character. Yet she would not really have had it any other way.

'There is,' thought Leah, 'very great satisfaction in doing one's best for those whom one loves.'

CHAPTER EIGHT

'We will be drawing into the station in just a moment,' Leah said. 'Marie Regina has no railway terminus. There was a proposal at one time to run the line almost through the village, but my father opposed it vigorously, and the trains follow a loop line that only comes within three miles of the estate. Ah! here we are! And there is John. He promised to meet me.'

'Does he know–?' Grace ventured.

'I've already explained to you,' Leah said patiently, 'that I told my brother I would be returning with a young lady.'

'You were very sure that I'd agree,' Grace said slowly.

'My dear, I seldom embark on an enterprise unless I am certain of the outcome,' Leah said dryly. 'Your valise is not too heavy for you, is it?'

Grace shook her head and mentally braced herself as the train drew up alongside a platform on which a gentleman stood, hat in hand.

Her first impression was one of familiarity, for John Falcon was very much like Price in colouring, though slimmer in build. His eyes betrayed no more than a well-bred curiosity as he bowed over her hand, but lit into affection as he kissed his sister's cheek.

'Did Price get off all right?' he asked, signalling a lounging porter to take the two small trunks to the pony trap that stood in the lane beyond.

'With no trouble at all. He was beginning to use nautical expressions even before visitors had come ashore,' Leah smiled.

'And this is Miss Finn?' He turned again to Grace, repeating the name Leah had murmured.

'You had best call her Grace,' Leah said. This was the moment when, if Price had ever mentioned his mistress, John might recall the name, but his face showed no recognition.

As they climbed up to the trap, John said, 'Does Grace – is she aware of the proposed arrangement?'

'She knows that you wish to take a wife and have entrusted me with the task of introducing a suitable young lady,' Leah said smoothly. 'Of course, the final decision is between the two of you.'

'Oh, I'm sure she'll suit very well,' John said vaguely, gathering up the reins.

Inwardly he was both elated and startled. He had not expected Leah to produce such a handsome piece, and he was gravely doubtful about his ability to please such a woman.

'Grace is a member of the theatrical profession,' Leah said brightly. 'It might be as well to give the girls the impression that you have been friendly for several months.'

'In what productions have you appeared?' John enquired. Grace answered mechanically, her attention caught by the flower-starred meadows, the distant woodlands, the faint thread of blue that wound like a ribbon between green banks.

'We take the bridle road through the south meadow,' John said, turning the trap expertly into a wide, mossy track. 'The other way is along the main road. It bisects Falcon land from the village itself.'

'Where does the estate start?' Grace asked.

'We're on Falcon land now,' Leah said.

'It's not an enormous estate,' John said. 'A thousand acres, but it stretches down to the river and beyond to an equal extent. And it's good growing land – wheat, hops, and cider apples mainly. We used to be largely self-supporting. The deerpark is rather fine. We limit the hunting so as not to deplete the stock. You can see Kingsmead ahead of us, behind the trees. We're coming to the courtyard wall now.'

They had emerged into a tree-lined drive and were approaching an archway in an ivied wall. Grace had a moment's panic as if invisible doors had clanged behind her, and then they had drawn up in a cobbled yard, and a groom stepped out to take the reins as John assisted the two women to alight.

The house was bigger than Grace had imagined and it looked very old. It looked, she thought, staring at it in nervous fascination, as if it had always been there and would remain long after all trace of human occupation had vanished.

'Welcome to Kingsmead,' John said cordially, and Leah took her arm and led her up some shallow steps, through an enormous open door, into a great hall that rose high above her head, and was shadowed by tapestries that rustled in the slight breeze from the courtyard.

'This was originally the great hall,' John said. 'The family ate here, as we still do, and sat here in the evenings. It hasn't been altered since the sixteenth century.'

'It's very interesting,' Grace said faintly. Her own tastes ran to fluffy cushions and thick rugs, and the stone floor and staircase, the heavy dark furniture and greyish tapestries depressed her.

'The two wings were built on later,' Leah was saying. 'The entire building is like the letter E with the middle bar missing, you see. Edith! Beth!'

She raised her voice and two figures appeared almost simultaneously from a door on the left.

'Girls, I have brought a visitor home with me, a friend of John's,' Leah continued. 'You had better come and greet her.'

She spoke, Grace thought, as if they were children, though the taller of the two was obviously in her twenties, the younger about sixteen.

'My sisters, Edith and Elizabeth,' Leah said. 'Miss Grace Finn.'

They shook hands politely, but Grace was aware of their surprise. Evidently unexpected visitors were rare at Kingsmead. She was also aware of the contrast between their elegantly simple gowns and her own feather trimmed jacket and fringed bustle.

'You never told us,' said Edith reproachfully, 'that anybody was coming.'

145

'My dear Edith, I am not obliged to give you advance warning of every action I intend to take,' Leah said pleasantly. 'Beth, will you take Grace up to the pink guestroom? She will wish to tidy herself before tea.'

'I'll get your trunk sent up,' John said. Grace murmured her thanks and followed the younger girl up the wide staircase to the railed gallery above. She could see a long line of portraits against the wall, but Beth turned to the right, opened a door which led into a narrow, right-angled corridor and indicated the first of two doors.

'This is the pink room, Miss Finn. I'll have Annie bring some hot water for you. We'll be downstairs when you're ready.'

She gave a friendly, slightly crooked smile and whisked out.

Grace unpinned her toque and looked round, noting with relief that a thick carpet covered the floor and that the walls were panelled in pale wood. The curtains at the window were of pink brocade with tiny silver flowers on them, and a matching quilt was spread over the bed. The general effect was cheerful and welcoming, though the absence of sheets under the quilt and the emptiness of the crystal vase proved that no visitor had been expected. Leah had certainly intended

146

to surprise the rest of the family.

A rosy-cheeked servant brought in hot water and towels, bobbed a curtsey and withdrew.

Grace's spirits began to rise. The great hall had depressed her, but this part of the house was furnished more in the style she had fancied the gentry preferred. When she had washed her hands and removed her jacket, she risked a quick peep into the adjoining room, and found it furnished in blue.

The walls of Kingsmead were so thick, that few sounds penetrated them. The silence began to get on her nerves. She was used to the constant rumble of wheeled traffic, the cries of street hawkers, and this quietness closed in about her.

She went out into the main gallery again. From here she could look down into the hall. A maid, the same one who had brought the water, crossed, staggering under the weight of an enormous silver tray, piled with utensils for tea. From a doorway at the other end of the gallery a man emerged.

His face was in shadow, but he saw her at once and gave a decided start.

'I beg your pardon. I was on my way down for tea,' she said quickly. 'My name is Grace Finn. I'm a friend of Lord – of John's.'

'I beg *your* pardon.' He lengthened his stride, reached her and shook hands. 'For a moment I thought Lady Regina had stepped out of her frame.'

'Lady Regina?'

'Regina Falcon, one of the most colourful of my wife's ancestors. I'm Paul Simmons, Leah's husband.'

'The writer?'

'In a small way as yet. I'm working on my first novel.'

'I was an actress. Musical comedy,' she confided.

'Was?'

'I've retired,' Grace said primly.

'Isn't it rather early for you to be considering retirement?' he asked, amused.

'I may be getting married,' she said.

'Then congratulations are due for the fortunate gentleman,' Paul said.

'Am I really like the Lady Regina?' she asked with interest.

'Superficially. She had red hair and an opulent figure too.'

His tone was slightly more familiar than it would have been talking to a lady. Grace, instead of resenting it, felt a faint comradely warmth. Here was one member of the family to whom she could talk on equal terms.

'What did Lady Regina do?' she asked.

'Come and look at her.' He led the way to one of the portraits and nodded at it. 'She was born during the Civil War, officially the daughter of Sir Robin Falcon and his wife, Charity.'

'Officially?'

'It's an open secret that her real father was Robin's brother Hal. She seems to have inherited some of her father's wildness. Tradition has it that she became the King's mistress and obtained a peerage for her son. What's the matter? Don't you like the picture?'

'She was very beautiful,' Grace said, looking at the sleepy green eyes, long auburn ringlets, and half-exposed curves of the woman in Restoration costume, 'but what a shocking story.'

'My wife would agree with you. It's not a tale she cares to have repeated,' Paul said. 'Shall we go down to tea?'

He offered her his arm, again with the slightly too-familiar air, and they walked down into the hall together, and through the door on the right into a long, high-ceilinged apartment, elegantly draped in rose and apricot. French windows at the end of the room looked out over close-clipped lawns and beds of roses. There were roses arranged in bowls in the room itself, and tea was laid out on a round table.

The others were already there, Edith and Beth side by side on a couch, John in an armchair, Leah in a high-backed wing chair near the table. She looked up as they came in and said,

'So you've introduced yourselves. Come and have some tea, Grace. You must be tired after your journey. I have been telling the girls the good news.'

'News?' Grace asked.

'Your engagement to John.' Leah poured tea, passed two cups. 'I kept my promise to John to say nothing until you were actually here, but I couldn't keep the news to myself any longer.'

'We must write and tell Price,' Edith said. 'I do think that John could have told us before Price left.'

'I will tell Price all in good time,' Leah said calmly. 'If we tell him too soon he is quite likely to rush home again. Much better to allow him to get settled out there. We are talking of my younger brother, Grace, the one who has just sailed to South Africa. He is hoping to go into the diamond business. I suppose John has mentioned him?'

'Yes. Oh, yes,' Grace said.

'When is the marriage to be?' Paul asked.

'John intends to apply for a special licence,' Leah said, 'and have a very simple ceremony in about ten days' time. Ostentatious weddings are going out of fashion, I'm told.'

'Engagement rings too, it seems,' Paul said.

'I didn't want one,' Grace said, a shade too quickly. 'I'm superstitious about engagement rings.'

'I still think Price ought to have been told,' Edith said. 'It's not every day that John gets married.'

'Where did you meet?' Paul enquired.

'Apparently John took an evening off in order to visit the theatre,' Leah said. 'Grace was playing a small role, but she seems to have eclipsed the star of the show in John's eyes.'

'I never knew you were such a sly fox, John,' Paul said. 'You keep a lovely girl like that under wraps for so long. I congratulate you. It will be interesting to have an actress in the family.'

'New blood is always welcome,' said Leah. 'Beth have you lost your wits? What in the world are you staring at?'

'A lady with red hair,' Beth said.

Visions of a crystal, seen dimly in mist, of a sword suspended over three women, hovered in her mind, and she was cold with terror.

'Beth, what on earth are you babbling about?' Leah said sharply.

'My sister is forever in a dream world,' John said.

'And constantly forgets her manners,' Leah said. 'Grace, you must have some of the seed-cake. It is Cook's pride and joy. And afterwards John will want to show you over the rest of the house.'

It was, thought Grace, like being in a play and not knowing one's lines or how the plot was supposed to work out. She was trapped among people who either believed lies about her or were using her. The girl, Beth, had a queer, dazed look on her face as if she had seen something horrible.

Tea over, Grace was taken on the proposed tour of Kingsmead. John was obviously very proud of his home, and glad of the opportunity of showing it off. Despite herself she was interested in what he said, for something of his own enthusiasm began to infect her as he pointed out the handsome baptismal cup presented to a long ago Falcon by the first Queen Elizabeth, showed her the lute in the solar, with the tapestry frame set up in the parlour, the table in the great hall at which generations of Falcon had sat.

Neither was Kingsmead as confusing as she had thought. In the old, main part of the house the kitchen and stillroom opened off one side of the main hall, with solar and parlour opening off the other side. There was a study and the bedroom occupied by Leah and her husband over the two latter rooms, and John slept in one of the two bedrooms over the kitchens. The guest rooms were in one of the wings over the servants' quarters. The opposite wing consisted of the enormous drawing-room where they had had tea, with a correspondingly large bedroom above it shared by Edith and Beth.

'We have been thinking of having bathrooms installed,' John said, leading Grace across the main hall again and ushering her into the courtyard. 'My sister will see to it, I've no doubt. She is very busy at the moment with the proposed school-building. "Proposed" is not quite the right word. The main building is almost completed. Of course the workmen have been aided by this long spell of fine weather, and Leah keeps them up to the mark.'

Grace could easily believe it.

'This is the old well,' John was saying, 'but we still get our drinking water from it. There are other wells on the east side with a piped system to the kitchen area. Eventually steps will be taken to link us up with the main water supply, but these things take time.'

'I am not going to buy the house, you know,' Grace said.

John flushed uncomfortably and fiddled with a bit of creeper on the wall. His voice, when he spoke, held all the self-doubt of a nervous and shy young man.

'It must seem very odd, very eccentric of me to ask my sister to find me a wife. I mean, there are young girls I already know, daughters of local families and so on, but the truth is that I've never been much at my ease with any of them. Price could always cut a dash with the ladies, even when he was still at school, but I never could think of anything to say to them.'

'Your sister said that you were very busy,' Grace said.

'Oh yes, indeed!' He seized upon her remark with relief. 'The estate requires a great deal of attention, and then I feel it obligatory to attend sittings in the Lords fairly regularly. Not that I've made my maiden speech yet. So when Leah suggested she introduce me to a young lady.'

His words trailed away. Grace, looking at him, wondered what else he was concealing. Aloud, she said, repeating the words she and Leah had rehearsed in the train.

'I hope you don't mind my having been on the stage. I was on the verge of giving it all up when I first met your sister. We were both buying hats, if you please, and fell into conversation. I mentioned I'd some old dresses I was going to donate to charity, and she told me she did some charity work from time to time, and took down my address. That was about a year ago, and I forgot all about it, until I saw her again just recently.'

He remembered vaguely that Leah had gone up to town to buy some dresses the previous summer, ready for when they took off mourning. She had not mentioned falling into conversation with anybody.

'You must have been very surprised at the proposal she made to you,' he said.

'Knocked all of a heap!' Grace said truthfully, and gave him an almost maternal look.

Innocent as a babe, for all his title and his fine estate! He was, being male, fortunately unaware that Grace and Leah were scarcely likely to patronize the same milliner. He was

155

being so trusting, prepared to believe any tale his sister cared to invent.

'We thought it better to give the rest of the family the impression that we'd been keeping company together for some time,' John said.

They had strolled in through the archway and were walking slowly down the main drive.

'To tell you the truth I didn't expect Leah to find somebody so quickly,' he said. 'She said she would be bringing a young lady back with her, but I didn't take it too seriously.'

'I think your sister usually means what she says.'

'Oh, Leah is splendid!' he agreed enthusiastically. 'She has always been the practical, clever one, and though she is devoted to the family she has no notions about having to marry within one's own class.'

'New blood in the family,' Grace said, and shivered.

'Old established families are apt to get a little insular,' said John. 'But Leah went and married a journalist fellow – he's writing a book, you know. And Price has taken himself off to the ends of the earth to make his fortune, and here I am about to marry a musical-comedy actress.'

'In ten days' time,' Grace said dryly.

'I had not planned,' John said awkwardly, 'on having the wedding so soon. I think it's a little unfair of Leah not to have given you a little more time, to get accustomed to Kingsmead. I assume that you are city-bred, and life in the country is very quiet. We don't entertain very often, I'm afraid.'

'I've always longed to live in the country,' Grace said.

At that moment she believed sincerely that she was speaking the truth.

'And the house? You do like the house?'

'It's a beautiful house!' Grace cried. 'And all this land! As far as I can see and beyond.'

'I'm afraid the Falcons got rich in the beginning on land confiscated from the monasteries,' John said wryly. 'However we have tried to do our best for the villagers. Much remains to be done, of course. Some of the tied cottages are extremely insanitary; and it's a scandal that we have never had a school. Even that will be remedied very soon.'

'Will your sister – I suppose she and her husband will be moving to the new school?'

'Lord, no!' John looked at her in astonishment. 'Why would they move? Kingsmead is

Leah's home, and as Paul has resigned his newspaper work in order to concentrate on his novel, then it makes little difference to him where he lives.'

'I see.'

'Not that Leah will interfere with us,' John said earnestly. 'She is always willing to suggest, to help, but she leaves us free. Upon my soul, but it hurt her, I'm sure of it, when Price decided to go abroad. Mind you, she didn't say a word. That's not her way. She helped in the preparations and saw him off; as happy as a sandboy he was, I understand.'

Happy to be free of his debts, and escape from his responsibilities, Grace thought, and was suddenly furious. It would serve Price right if he returned home to find his discarded mistress in possession of it.

'If it isn't too much trouble,' she said, 'I don't mind being wed in ten days' time. That is, if you'll think I'd suit.'

She wished she did not sound as if she were begging for a job as parlourmaid.

'I think we'd suit very well,' John said. 'It's not as if we start out with all kinds of romantic illusions. You like Kingsmead and I need a wife, and we'd rub along very comfortably together. Leah will tell you that I'm fairly amiable, not demanding.'

Grace was sorry for him without knowing exactly why. There was, she sensed, a weakness in him, but where that weakness lay or how it might be cured she had no idea.

'We shall all get along very well,' he was continuing, as they began to retrace their steps along the drive. 'My other sisters are both friendly creatures. You mustn't take any notice of Beth's fancies. She is what people call "fey" but we don't take things too seriously in our family. And Edith can be moody, but that will come right when she's found herself a husband.'

They were passing under the archway, and he broke off as Edith herself drifted towards them. She was, thought Grace without envy, quite incredibly lovely, her pale golden hair wound unfashionably but effectively around her ears, her long-lashed blue eyes sweetly solicitous.

'Leah was worried lest you take cold,' she said. 'It's gone quite chilly, and you've no jacket or shawl on, so I was coming to find you.'

She herself wore a white shawl and the breeze lifted its ends like wings.

Grace, looking past her, saw Paul Simmons standing by the well-head. Leah's husband was looking at Edith too.

CHAPTER NINE

'This is wrong,' Edith whispered, but her words were lost in the hollow between Paul's chin and shoulder. 'Oh, my love, we ought not to be here like this!'

'Then run away. Go home.' He spoke sleepily, casually, but his arm pressed her tightly against him, and her eyes closed again in contentment.

'We will have to go home soon,' she said reluctantly. 'I am supposed to be in the church, arranging flowers for the Harvest Thanksgiving service.'

'Leah won't be very pleased when she sees the empty vases.'

'They won't be empty, Beth said she'd do them for me. I told her I wanted to exercise the new gelding.'

'Won't Leah look in at the church?'

'Not she. Leah will be too busy hanging curtains up at the school to think about church decorations.'

'That wife of mine is always busy about something,' Paul said, and stretched lazily.

'Not so busy that she cannot find time to poke and pry into everybody's business,' Edith said bitterly. 'There is not a corner of my life where she doesn't put in her fingers and meddle!'

'Except this corner.' He cupped her bare breast in his hand and raised himself on an elbow to gaze down at her.

Even in the aftermath of love-making Edith retained her cool, languid beauty. Her long, pale hair flowed like silk over her white shoulders and only the faintest colour showed in her exquisitely modelled cheek-bones. It was a pity, thought Paul, that she was so stupid. He had always admired brains and wit in a woman, believing they lasted when physical beauty faded. Edith was undeniably beautiful, but she had nothing in her head except the pleasure of the moment, and her moods were shallow. He had seen her petulant and sulky. He had held her in the most intimate embrace of all and seen her smile with pleasure. But he had never heard her cry out in passion, never seen her face distorted in anger or desire.

'We ought not to be here,' she repeated. 'You're my sister's husband.'

'Is your conscience bothering you, my pet?' he enquired.

'I suppose it ought to bother me,' she said doubtfully, 'but it pleases me to think I have something of hers when she allows me nothing of my own.'

'You talk as if Leah owned me,' he said irritably.

'She tries to own everybody,' Edith said. 'Sometimes I think she won't be content until she has eaten us all up.'

'You will come into your ten thousand a year in a few months,' he said, with a touch of malice.

'And I will be twenty-five years old,' she said, and her face was suddenly sharp and bleak so that he saw her as she might look in old age, her beauty gone and only the beautiful bones remaining. 'I will be twenty-five years old, Paul, and still unwed.'

'But not untouched, eh?'

'No, indeed! She has not succeeded in denying me that,' Edith said with satisfaction. 'She has not succeeded in keeping her husband faithful.'

'I am not the faithful kind,' Paul said.

'Is that a warning?' She wriggled away and swung her legs over the side of the bed.

'You're very pretty, and very foolish,' he said lightly. 'Come back to bed.'

'I want to get dressed. Help me with my corsets.'

'I cannot imagine how you women can bear to wear these,' Paul said, moving to obey.

'Don't pull it too tightly,' Edith admonished. 'I shall have to let it out a little.'

'You're putting on weight.' He slapped her lightly on the rump and said again, in a different tone, 'You're putting on weight!'

'I was always too slender,' Edith said, reaching for her skirt. 'Beth now is inclined to plumpness, but then she is forever raiding the pantry.'

'When did you last have your monthly courses?' he demanded.

'My monthly – Paul, don't be so indelicate!' she exclaimed.

'When?' he repeated.

'I don't know. Last month, two months ago.'

'Is that usual? Are you sometimes irregular?'

'No. No. I don't think so. Paul, a gentleman shouldn't know about such – oh, my God! you don't think that I'm with child!'

She sat down again on the edge of the bed, her hand over her mouth, her blue eyes wide with fear.

'Probably not. Probably not.' His voice

163

was uneasy.

'But it could have happened,' she whispered. 'I might be going to have your child. Oh, Paul, what will Leah say?'

A picture of Leah, clear-eyed, tight-lipped, rose in his mind.

'She will never forgive me,' Edith said. 'She will drive me away from Kingsmead.'

'But you're always telling me that you hate this place, that you want to go and live in London,' he protested.

'But not with a child. Not with a bastard child.'

'We must be mistaken,' he said hopefully.

'Do you think so? Perhaps I muddled the dates, and I'm getting plump because I've been eating more than usual. And even if it were true, you'd think of something. You'd take care of me.'

She had recovered her serenity and her voice was trustful.

Trustful and stupid, Paul thought. She was beginning to bore him.

'You aren't *afraid* of Leah, are you?' Edith asked suddenly.

'Afraid of her? That's a ridiculous statement.' He had begun to dress, his movements jerky, his face sombre.

'Is it?' Edith put on her bodice and

164

fastened it. 'You don't love her. You didn't marry her because you loved her.'

'She's an interesting woman,' he said.

'She's cold-hearted and possessive,' Edith contradicted. 'You said that making love to her was like making love to a wax doll.'

'Yes.'

'You said that you had made a terrible mistake and that I was the one you loved.'

'I said a great many things,' Paul said wearily.

'If it's money,' Edith said brightly, 'I'll have my own in a few months. You could still write your book. I might be able to help you with it. I could number the pages or something.'

'We'll think of something, if the worst comes to the worst.'

He was cold with apprehension, but Edith had regained her poise. The fear of pregnancy had already been shelved, and she was making plans like a child.

'I shall wait a few weeks, until I am certain one way or the other, and then we will decide what to do,' she said, combing her hair and beginning to plait it. 'If I could contrive to hide it until my birthday.'

'The child would be born before your birthday,' he said brusquely.

'Then we will have to think of something

else.' She coiled one long plait over her ear and smiled. 'You're very clever, darling. You'll think of something.'

'Don't you understand,' he said, through clenched teeth, 'that this is a serious matter? If you're – all hell will be let loose!'

'Yes, Leah will be absolutely furious!' She gave a nervous giggle, the colour returning to her face.

It was useless. One might as well be angry with a child. Edith was, in many ways, no more than a rather greedy child, enjoying the pleasures of the moment, pushing away trouble for a more convenient time.

'We can live together,' she was saying now, pinning up her other plait. 'They can't stop me from having my money. We could change our names and live in London or Paris. I've always wanted to visit Paris.'

'No sense in making up our minds now,' he said, watching her as she tied on her small, velvet hat.

'As you say, there's plenty of time. I'll go back by the main road. You wait a while and then stroll back through the fields. Isn't it lucky that Beth never keeps this cottage locked!'

'Very lucky,' he said dully, and kissed her mechanically. His desire for her had fled as completely as if it had never been. Her beauty once enjoyed had begun to pall, and the childishness that had been so enchanting was, he saw, no more than the reflection of her stupidity. The idea of living with her, of trying to write while she chattered of unimportant matters, appalled him. Leah was indifferent to his occasional caresses, but she did not cloy like treacle. Edith was too soft and too willing, and when he was not making love to her he could not raise the slightest interest in anything she had to say.

'I'm sure everything will be all right,' she was saying. 'There really isn't any point in crossing bridges before we come to them, is there?'

'No indeed,' he agreed, and felt intense relief as she blew a kiss and went lightly out of the room and down the stairs.

He heard her mount up and the brisk clip-clop of hoofs along the bridle path. Then the cottage was tranquil again, save for the fluting of birds beyond the latticed windows and the rushing of the river.

Paul sat down and put his head in his hands. It had been sheer insanity to begin the affair with Edith at all, but since the birth of John and Grace's son, Leah had been more preoccupied than ever. It was not that he particularly missed his wife's company, but the long, lazy hours in the study where he had read and smoked and made occasional additions to his novel, had been spoiled by the wailing of a child, by constant interruptions as Leah came in and out to fetch one thing and another. He had sought to escape into the spring-blossoming fields and woodlands, and found Edith willing to bear him company. She was beautiful and yielding, and as he made love to her part of him thought, in spiteful triumph, that it served Leah right. She made it so obvious, in a hundred subtle ways, that she had stooped from a lofty pedestal in order to honour him with her hand.

But if Edith were expecting his child, summer dalliance would become winter despair. Leah would not endure such a situation. He and Edith would be driven away, and he would not only lose the comforts of Kingsmead, but would be saddled with a woman for whom he felt only physical desire and an unwanted child.

He rose, glancing round the tiny bedroom, and went down the stairs. The cottage had become a regular trysting place for him and

Edith, and there was little danger of their being discovered, for only Beth ever went near the house, and they usually made certain that she was occupied elsewhere at those times.

He closed the front door and stood for a moment in the clearing. This part of the estate had been left to run wild apart from the occasional efforts that Beth made to cut back the creepers. She looked after the cottage herself rather as if it were a large dolls' house, but the bushes and trees pressed closely about the green space and the bridle path was overgrown with bramble and ivy.

He was about to stroll along the path in preparation for the walk back to Kingsmead through the meadows when a rustling from the direction of the river halted him. For an instant the fear that Leah had hidden in order to spy upon him clutched him, but then a tousled figure pushed through into the clearing and stopped short in evident confusion.

'We always seem to be astonishing each other,' Paul said.

He spoke easily but warily, not feeling certain how much she had seen. Grace, however, was far too embarrassed about her own untidiness to pay any heed to the reason for his being there. Her red hair was tumbling down and her stockings and shoes were bundled under her arm. Under the tucked up hem of her skirt two soaking wet feet were displayed.

'It was so cool in the river that I couldn't resist taking a dip,' she said. 'I'm supposed to be on my way to the school to help Leah with the curtains, but I left the trap up on the bridge, and sneaked down.'

'I won't tell,' he said.

Evidently she had been too busy splashing in the river to hear Edith depart.

'I'd better dry my feet,' she said, looking at them with renewed confusion.

'Beth keeps towels in the cottage. I'll get you one.'

'I'll wait here,' Grace said, sitting on a large flat stone. 'That place gives me a creepy feeling.'

Paul hurried back into the living-room, snatched a towel from the hook at the back of the door, and came out again to find Grace pinning up her hair.

'Keep still! I'll dry them,' he said, and knelt to his task.

'Makes me feel like Cleopatra,' Grace said.

'She bathed in asses' milk,' he told her.

'Well, that sort of woman anyway.' She wriggled her toes and grinned, her embarrassment fading.

'What decided you to go wading?' he enquired.

It was the kind of thing Beth might take it into her head to do, but Grace had always behaved with nervous correctness.

'I wanted to feel free,' she said.

Paul gave her ankles a final rub and stood up. There were bits of grass in the red curls on the top of her head and he began to pick them out.

'What are you doing down here?' she asked in her turn.

'Perhaps I wanted to feel free too,' he said.

'Kingsmead is – it weighs you down a bit, don't you think?'

'I know what you mean,' he gazed at her bent head curiously and said,

'You're not happy are you?'

'I've every reason to be,' Grace said with a touch of defiance. 'John's a good, kind man. He worships me.'

That was true, Paul thought. John had evidently done his duty by the girl and made an honest woman of her, if her so-called seven month child were anything to go by. It was also evident that he loved her deeply.

His eyes followed her about with an expression in them almost of gratitude.

'And you have a fine baby,' he prompted.

She nodded and burst out, as if the words could no longer be contained.

'Teddy doesn't seem like my baby at all sometimes. Leah takes such good care of him as if she'd been looking after babies all her life. When I nurse him he struggles and yells. He doesn't even look like me. He looks much more like her!'

'Does it bother you to have Leah take charge?' he asked.

'She's very kind,' Grace said. 'I really can't complain when she works so hard and takes all the burden off my shoulders. She's very kind.'

'Yes,' he agreed.

They contemplated Leah's kindness in gloomy silence.

'And babies aren't very exciting, are they?' Grace said at last. 'You know, it's not a very nice thing to say, but I find Teddy awfully boring.'

'And Kingsmead? Is that boring too?'

Grace bit her lip, but the stage had been set for frankness, and her words rushed out.

'I really thought I'd enjoy living in the country. It's so pretty and the air's so clean and I thought there'd be picnics and harvest suppers and balls, but there isn't anything. John only leaves the estate when he has to go to the House of Lords, and no company ever comes. Day after day is exactly like the one before it with nothing different except the weather.'

'John ought to take you away somewhere for a few weeks,' Paul said. 'You didn't have a honeymoon, did you?'

'No. No honeymoon.' She began to laugh as if the phrase amused her. 'No honeymoon!'

Her white skin had flushed and tears shone in her eyes. Half-angry, half-amused, she gasped.

'Turn your back! I want to put on my stockings and shoes!'

He turned his back obediently hearing the rustle of her skirt in the grass, the soft hiss of silk being pulled over bare flesh.

'Damnation!' she swore. 'I beg your pardon!'

'What's wrong?'

'I've lost one of my garters,' she said in exasperation.

'It's here.' He picked the circle of white lace from the grass and went towards her with it, saying, 'Honi soit qui mal y pense.'

'That's Latin or Greek, isn't it? What does it mean?' she frowned.

'It means "evil be to him who evil thinks", or in other words, "It is the finder's right to put it where it belongs"?'

'I don't believe you,' she said, but she giggled as she spoke and stuck out her leg.

His hands, slipping the garter over her foot and up her calf, lingered on the silk.

'I get bored in the country too,' he said softly. 'But you're clever! You're writing a book,' she said.

'A good one. But this isn't the place to do it. I need challenge and stimulation.'

Her thigh was warm and shapely. His fingers kneaded the silk-swathed flesh and, glancing up, he saw that her blue eyes were half-closed, her breasts rising and falling rapidly.

'John doesn't – care about things like that,' she said jerkily. 'He makes a plaster saint of me to sit in the corner on a high shelf.'

'And you're one for–?'

'A bit of slap and tickle!' she said, and opened her eyes, wide and merry. 'But if you go tickling too high I'll have to start the slapping, won't I? So don't go thinking you can take liberties.'

'I wouldn't dream of it.' He took his hand

away and stood up, watching as she bent to pull on her shoes.

There was more spice in this girl than in Edith. She would be harder to conquer, and once won, more fun to occupy. There was a robustness about her that reminded him of the women seen in his own childhood, half-remembered figures in gay, grubby hats and tattered shawls who sang brave, jolly songs as they minced along the street on the way to earn a night's doss. His parents had tried to pretend that such women didn't exist.

'I tried so hard to like it here,' Grace said, abruptly forlorn. 'But I don't fit in, and there's the truth of it. I don't belong here any more than I belong on the moon. I'm only twenty-one and that's too young to be buried. I know it's ungrateful of me but I can't help myself. If they were mean or unkind it'd be better in a way, I'd have something to fight against, you see. But I don't belong here, and that's the whole trouble!'

'No more do I,' Paul said and put out his hand to help her rise. 'You and I are cuckoos in the nest, my dear girl.'

'At least we can be friends,' she said.

'As a beginning.' He squeezed her arm, noting the emerald brooch at her throat, the diamond ear-bobs. Lord Falcon, whatever his shortcomings in other directions, was evidently a generous husband.

'I'd not want to hurt John,' she said nervously. 'He's very good to me in lots of ways you know.'

'He neglects you.'

'Well, he's got responsibilities,' she said.

'How fortunate,' Paul said, 'that I have none.'

'I'd best be off to help Leah,' Grace said.

'By all means! go and enliven your day by hanging curtains,' he teased. 'What colour are they, by the way?'

'Brown,' Grace told him. 'I thought a nice pink would be gay, but Leah said that brown would be more practical.'

'And Leah, as usual, is probably right.'

He took her arm and chatted pleasantly as they left the clearing. At the bridge they separated, Grace climbing up into the pony-trap to continue her drive to the school, Paul striking across the meadows.

Later, Beth, having completed the flower arrangements to her satisfaction, came into the clearing and spotted the damp, crumpled towel. Somebody had evidently borrowed it and neglected to return it to the cottage. She picked it up, looked with disfavour at the mud stains on it, and went into the little house herself. There was time to rinse out the towel before she went home. Leah and Grace were busy hanging curtains and Edith was out riding. John had gone over to Maidstone to see about some repairs to Paget Place, a house in the town that was Falcon property. Paul would be writing or out walking. Beth was not much interested in Paul.

As she wrung out the towel the feeling that something in the cottage was different came over her. It must be, she thought, because she knew that somebody had it in her absence to borrow the towel. The event was unusual, but the feeling was not. She had had the same feeling several times recently when she had visited 'Witch's Dower'.

She frowned, wondering who had been here. The rest of the family were not interested in going there, the villagers shunned it, and it was too well hidden for casual passers-by to stumble upon it, even if casual passers-by had been in the habit of roaming about on Falcon land.

There was something else in the cottage too. She wrinkled up her nose and sniffed. The door to the herb-room was closed but this was not the smell of any herb. It was faintly but unmistakably violets. But violets grew in the springtime, not in the golden heart of summer.

Edith wore violet perfume. Leah had commented on it the previous day, remarking with lifted eyebrows, that the scent was too strong and clung to everything.

But Edith was out riding, and in any case she disliked 'Witch's Dower'. She'd referred to it more than once as 'Beth's mousehole', and declared that nothing on earth would induce her to go there alone.

Beth shrugged her shoulders and dismissed the matter from her mind. At eighteen she still possessed a child's gift of blotting out what didn't concern her, but like a child she saw and understood more than people realized.

She knew that John loved Grace very much, but that Grace didn't love John more than she might have loved a dear friend. She knew that Leah was beginning to be happy, though there had been long months when she had not been happy at all. She knew that Edith hated living at Kingsmead but was afraid to break away, and she knew that Paul was unhappy too, because he had no more affection for Leah than Grace had for John.

'When I meet my lover,' Beth told herself, 'I will know him at once and I will never love anyone else in my whole life. I will never marry for any reason, except love.'

Marriage was frequently in her mind these days. There had been a time when she had contemplated the notion of spinsterhood with very little dismay, but her mirror showed her a face and figure from which the chubbiness was beginning to melt, and had it not been for Leah's dislike of city life, she would by now have had her London season. Beth, pulling her tail of hair upwards and fluttering her long eyelashes at herself in the round mirror on the wall began to practise being a society belle and forgot about violet perfume.

CHAPTER TEN

'If we could only have a dinner-party,' Edith said restlessly, 'I'm sure it would liven us up.'

'You must speak for yourself,' Leah said, 'for I certainly don't feel myself to be in any need of – livening-up. Why, it's hardly a week since we attended the harvest supper, and in another ten days we have the official opening of the school.'

'That will be Grace's task, as Lady Falcon,' Edith said.

'Of course, if dear Grace considers herself equal to the task,' Leah smiled.

'No, oh no!' Grace flushed miserably and crumpled the bread on her plate. 'I have had nothing to do with any of it! I think you ought to open the school, Leah.'

'If you truly think so. I suppose as the eldest Falcon it would be appropriate.'

'It seems rather strange,' John said quietly reflective, 'to be opening a school when we have not yet appointed a school-mistress. We have had no joy from our advertisement, have we, Leah?'

'And that, my dear brother,' said Leah, with an air of triumph, 'is where you are mistaken in part. I grant you that those who answered the advertisement were unsuitable, but we have a teacher nonetheless.'

'Oh? Who?' John looked interested.

'You remember Great-Aunt Catrin?' asked Leah.

'Mam's aunt, the one who brought her up? The one who lives in Wales?' Beth enquired.

'As Mam had only one aunt it's not likely I'd be referring to anybody else,' Leah said.

'We've never seen her,' Edith remarked. 'You're not saying that she's coming to teach here!'

'Great-Aunt Catrin has lived on a farm since she was born, and is not likely to leave it now,' Leah said with a touch of asperity. 'But I received a letter from her some weeks ago, informing me that her daughter had recently been widowed and naturally wishes for a change of scene to help soften her grief.'

'I never heard of her daughter before,' Edith said, 'Is she a cousin or what?'

'You have certainly heard her mentioned,' Leah said, 'but as you take neither pride nor interest in the family, you failed to remember. Wenna is, strictly speaking, Mam's cousin, but she is very much younger. Great-Aunt Catrin married fairly late on in life and bore her child in middle-age.'

'How old is this Wenna?' Beth enquired.

'*Cousin* Wenna is in her early twenties,' Leah said quellingly. 'Her husband was killed three months ago, about three weeks after their marriage. He worked in the local slate quarry and fell. Great-Aunt Catrin gave no details. However, I wrote at once, inviting the young lady to come on an extended visit, and mentioning the school.'

'You mean you offered her the post of teacher?' John asked in surprise.

'Not yet. I mean to engage her for a probationary period of six months,' Leah said calmly. 'I mentioned it, as a suggestion when I wrote, and received a reply from cousin Wenna herself. I must say the letter impressed me favourably. She writes a most respectable hand and expresses herself very gracefully.'

'I wish you had said something to me about this,' John said.

There was a mild displeasure in his face. Leah gave him a hurt, reproachful look.

'I wished to surprise you,' she said gently. 'If this – what was her married name? – ah, yes, Davies – if this Wenna Davies is not able to keep order or to impart knowledge then we will have to make other arrangements. But she is, albeit distant, a member of the family. Would it not be pleasant to have a member of the family living where the old manor used to stand?'

'And being a member of the family,' Grace said brightly, 'you could get her cheap!'

Beth giggled naughtily and Paul hastily took a mouthful of wine.

'Expense,' said Leah coldly, 'does not enter into the matter.'

'No, of course not! I only meant–' Grace floundered uncomfortably, aware that she had again said the wrong thing. Whenever Leah was present she invariably said the wrong thing. With relief she heard the thin wailing of the baby and rose.

'I'll go to Teddy,' Leah forestalled her neatly. 'The rest of you will excuse me. I'm sure. I don't want any dessert.'

She left the table and went with her smooth, unhurried step up the stairs. The baby was awake and wet, his fists beating the air angrily, his eyes screwed up. She changed him and lifted him against her shoulder, patting his plump back. His crying appeased, he curled his fingers blissfully into her smooth coils of hair and gurgled.

He was always, she thought, good when she held him. Grace had no notion how a baby should be held or nursed. Indeed Grace seemed to have little feeling either for the child or John. Leah, cuddling Teddy, wondered if her brother realized that his wife cared nothing for him. He had spoken little of his marriage except on one occasion just after Grace had announced her pregnancy. On that occasion he had said privately to Leah,

'It seems that you were right and the specialist wrong, but I cannot begin to understand it. I could have sworn that our marriage was not fully consummated!'

'I'll be bound that Grace didn't complain,' she said lightly.

'Grace is wonderful,' was all John said, but his eyes had glowed and Leah had heaved a small sigh of relief. Whatever Grace's opinions as to the reason behind her unconventional marriage, she was too kind-hearted to taunt John with them.

'And you, my little pet,' Leah said softly to the baby, 'will be Lord Falcon one day.'

Price's and Grace's son, and yet more Leah's than either of theirs, for Price was in South Africa and had sent home only two brief letters, and Grace had little interest in her baby.

'You're Aunt Leah's little darling, aren't you?' Leah crooned. 'You're going to be master of Kingsmead and marry a snow-white maiden.'

Teddy chortled in agreement and nuzzled her neck.

'Soon,' she whispered into his fuzz of dark hair, 'you'll have a little cousin, but we won't love it any more than we love you.'

Her own pregnancy was only two months advanced, and she had not yet told anybody. In a way the child she was carrying was unreal to her. She would be fond of it when it came, but she could not imagine having stronger feelings for it than she had for Teddy.

Stepping lightly and jogging the babe in a soothing rhythm that generally sent him back to sleep Leah went out to the gallery and began to pace up and down. Below in the great hall the family still sat at table, their heads gleaming under the candlelight, their voices mingling in conversation. It was odd, thought Leah, that they always seemed much more at ease when she was a little apart from them. It was a little lonely to realize such a thing and she shut down the thought and went along the gallery to her own rooms.

The lamps had already been lit in the study and they cast a warm, comforting radiance over the apartment. Leah went through into the bedroom and put Teddy down in the middle of the bed. He snuggled down in the quilt and promptly fell asleep.

Leah went back into the study and sat down by the desk, leaning her head against the high-backed leather chair. Although she would not have admitted it, she was weary. Apart from the school project and her charity work there were the normal running

185

of the household and the baby to attend.

But matters were going well. She had written to Price, not telling him of John's marriage. John himself never put pen to paper if he could avoid it and, of the others, only Edith had written. Fortunately, the mail being put on a tray in the solar for one of the servants to take into the village, it had been easy to remove Edith's letter from the pile. In the months since his departure Price had become vague and shadowy. No doubt he would settle down on the other side of the world and they would eventually lose contact with him. It was sad, but sacrifices had to be made if the family was to continue free of the taint of scandal.

As it was, John's self-respect had been saved and although Grace was a vulgar young woman there was no denying she was healthy and would bequeath a sturdy constitution to her son.

'And now,' Leah murmured aloud, 'I too am to have a child.'

The knowledge pleased her, made her feel complete. It was not often that Paul made love to her these days. She supposed that the physical aspects of marriage became less important as time went on. Certainly a lady would not complain of such a lack, just as she would not permit herself to display pleasure when her husband caressed her.

'Mental companionship is far more important,' Leah told herself, and glanced involuntarily at the locked desk. Two years was surely long enough in which to rewrite a novel. For two years Paul had spent part of every day at this desk, carefully locking away his writing when he left, and in all that time she had never asked if she might see what he had done. And in all that time she had supported him, bought his clothes, paid for the parcels of books that he ordered – her eyes flashed to the hook at the back of the door where his jacket hung. She had looked in the jacket before for the key, of course, and been disappointed, but some intuition made her rise and go to the jacket again, her slim fingers poking into the pockets. The key was there. She drew it out in surprised triumph. Paul had been absent-minded these past few days. She had spoken to him several times without receiving an answer, and he had frequently had a dreamy, irritatingly complacent look on his face. She clutched the key in the palm of her hand and went out to the gallery again.

Her voice floated down to them serenely.

'I think Teddy is cutting a tooth, so I'll

187

keep him with me tonight. Paul, would you ask Annie to make you up a bed in the spare room? You'll not want your sleep broken, will you?'

They were looking up at her and nodding agreement. Leah had the sudden, irrational conviction that she would never look at them in exactly the same way again, or that when she did they would have changed in some fundamental manner.

'I'll say good night then,' she said loudly, and a chorus of dutiful good nights echoed after her as she returned to the study, and softly drew the bolt on the door.

Teddy was still sleeping. She went back to the desk, inserted the small key in the lock, and twisted it. The deep drawer slid open and a pile of closely written manuscript pages were within her grasp.

Her hands trembled a little with excitement as she lifted them out. It might be that Paul was the genius she had hoped, and she was destined to be the one to lay the fruits of his labour before a waiting world.

The papers on the flat-topped desk before her, she took up the first one and began to read. For the next couple of hours she read steadily, and with an increasing sense of disappointment.

The book was evidently autobiographical, telling in minute and tedious detail the kind of rags to riches story she had often enjoyed in the novels of Charles Dickens. But Paul Simmons had no ear for dialogue, no gift for characterization. The words flowed out, not crystal clear, but lame and turgid, unlit by any spark of humour. As she went on she began to skip passages to read more quickly in an attempt to find some gleam of gold amid the dross.

It was in the eleventh chapter that her interest reawakened. The narrator of the tale, having failed to find recognition as an artist, had married an extremely silly woman for the sake of her money.

'Respectability was the keynote of her entire existence and the prospect of poking her nose into other folks' business her only expectation of pleasure. It was with increasing fervour that Peter began to pay attention to her fair young cousin, Selena. Their trysting place was a small cottage on the estate.'

But it was only a novel! All writers drew partly upon their own experiences, partly upon their imaginations, to create their plots.

Leah read now with painful intensity.

Ironically the style was improving as if a shaft of genuine passion pierced the lifeless words. The hero, Peter, was not only deceiving his wife but glorying in the deceit. He lived on her bounty, made love to her with distaste, and lived only for his hours with Selena whose perfume haunted him and whose white body stirred his senses.

The book was unfinished. Leah put down the last closely written sheet and gazed into space. Paul had married her for her money and the realization of that fact was no less bitter because deep down she had known it all along. Worse, having married her, he had proved unfaithful. She was certain that there was another woman, not only in the novel but in Paul's real life. A cousin. The only cousin of the Falcons was Wenna Davies who had not yet arrived.

But there were two sisters. Leah thought about each of them, coldly, analytically. Edith was languid and white skinned, but Beth had the crooked smile and the infectious laugh that was also mentioned. The exact colour of Selena's hair and eyes had not been stated.

Edith was jealous, resentful of the fact that Leah had a husband, and Edith had been Paul's first choice before Leah persuaded him that it would benefit him more if he married herself.

Beth was always down at the cottage, always wandering about with a dreaming look on her face. And she had those odd moods when she was not quite herself. In such a mood she might easily have been seduced.

'I will have to watch,' Leah thought. 'Accusation without proof is childish. I will have to watch carefully before I do anything. When I discover the truth, then I'll decide what to do. I knew something had turned him from me. I sensed it in my bones.'

She locked away the manuscript, and pressed the small key firmly into a wax tablet before returning it to the jacket. The next day she would ride over to Maidstone and have another key made. Then she would be able to read any additions Paul made to the manuscript. It was later than she had realized and the moon had risen. She went into the bedroom and closed the shutters, not allowing herself more than a brief glimpse at the silver crescent. What was it that Beth had once said? 'Do you ever wish on the moon, Leah?' Something like that. Wishing on the moon indeed! Or had Beth wished upon the moon and had Paul answered?

Teddy stirred and whimpered. Leah reached over, picked him up again and began to rock him in the familiar soothing rhythm. Her eyes, dry and burning, gazed unwinkingly into the darkness.

In the spare room Paul lay, willing sleep to come. There was, it seemed, little doubt that Edith was carrying his child. The knowledge angered him even though he acknowledged that anger to be irrational. Had he not seduced Edith she would never have become pregnant, but Edith had been more than willing. From his first coming to Marie Regina she had thrown herself at his head, and no man could be blamed for taking what was offered. Grace, for all her vulgarity, was infinitely more subtle. A man could make a comrade of Grace. He and she came from the same background and spoke the same language. Even hardship might be amusing with Grace to share it. He wished he had had the opportunity to see her on the stage. This quiet, country setting was not suited to her personality at all. Neither, he thought, was it suited to his own. The life of a country gentleman was becoming extremely tedious. There had been some sly, malicious pleasure in weaving the affair with Edith into the pages of his novel, but that part of the story would have to be altered before he could risk showing it to Leah, and in any case he had lost interest in the wretched book.

It was a waste of a good bed, he decided irritably to sleep in it alone, with Grace only just across the gallery. John, no doubt, would be asleep by now, leaving a space between himself and his red-headed wife. It was a mystery how he had ever managed to father that baby.

John in fact was snoring slightly as he drifted into sleep. It had been a long day with the final gleaning of the wheat to be supervised, two mares to be doctored, the furniture to be carted into the school. It was a little hurtful of Leah not to have consulted him regarding the arrival of their Welsh cousin, but she had wished to spare him trouble. Leah was splendid.

Grace, her vivid hair tied back, lay wakeful, trying to close her mind to the sound of John's snoring. He had kissed her good night and gone to sleep almost at once as he usually did. She was consumed with pity and contempt, pity because he would never fully play the part of a husband and contempt because he had allowed his sister to trick a girl into marriage with him.

At this moment Paul would be alone in the guest room a few yards away. Grace closed her eyes and Paul's face lean and sallow, hovered behind her eyelids. She had not meant to fall in love with him, but there was nothing for her to do at Kingsmead except sit at tapestry work with Edith, which she hated, or play with the baby who bored her, or accept chastely adoring kisses from John.

If only she could risk getting up and leaving the room and obeying the urge of her hungry flesh, but even though John was a heavy sleeper, there was always the risk that Leah might come out to the gallery. Leah moved too softly and her eyes were too sharp.

Edith was, like John, asleep. Her first panic at finding herself with child was subsiding. It was, after all, rather amusing to think she had outwitted Leah. And Paul would take care of her and the baby. In a few months time she would have ten thousand a year. The three of them could live on that, perhaps in Paris. It would be lovely to go to France with Paul. He could write books there, and perhaps some of that ten thousand a year could be spent on pretty dresses and jewels. John had bought Grace twenty thousand pounds' worth of gems. Grace, with typical low class manners, had boasted about it. A gentle smile on her delicate features, Edith dreamed of jewels and of Paul hanging them about her neck.

Beth was awake, and knowing instinctively that this was going to be a night when sleep came reluctantly, had slipped on a dressing gown and was curled up on the window-seat. Below her the lawns stretched to the deerpark, and the rose-bushes were tipped with silver. Against the moonlit sky every tree was sharply, blackly etched. High above the moon herself hovered in majesty.

One ought, Beth thought, to make a wish of some kind. The trouble was that it was selfish to wish for oneself, and yet Beth was not sure what each member of the family needed.

There was something odd going on among her elders. She had felt it for days, without knowing exactly what it was or even if it were good or bad. It was as if each person in the house had a secret, as if all the words they spoke had nothing to do with what they were really thinking.

She wished that she had her crystal, for she was in a mood to see things in it. When she did see things she looked, not through her eyes but from a point somewhere between her eyes, as if a screen had been drawn aside in her head and she could peer through and watch shadowy figures move there.

It was useless to try to sleep. She would, she decided, go down to the drawing-room and find a book. If she lit a candle she could curl up in her bed and read until her eyelids were heavy. She got down from the window sill, pushed her feet into a pair of slippers and padded out to the gallery.

The great hall was lit by shafts of moonlight that barred the stone floor. Beth went slowly down the stairs and into the drawing-room. The moonlight was shut out here by the heavy curtains of pink and apricot brocade. She crossed to the long windows and tugged at the silk cord that drew them back, and the pale light flooded through the apartment.

The mirrors reflected her image over and over as if a dozen Beths stood in the drawing-room, each one more ethereal than the last. In this room Falcon women in white wigs and hooped panniers had talked and drunk chocolate from tiny cups and flirted with gentlemen in satin breeches and velvet cloaks. Beth had read some of their names on the great family tomb. Eliza and Rosemary and – she closed her eyes and opened them quickly, as if she hoped to catch a glimpse of those vanished ladies.

A figure stood in the arched entrance, dark against moonwashed walls. Beth opened her mouth but before she could utter a sound Leah had strode forward, her voice harshly accusing.

'What are you doing here? What are you doing?'

'I came down to get a book,' Beth said, her voice high with relief.

Leah's hand shot out and fastened painfully on Beth's wrist.

'By moonlight? You intended to read by moonlight?'

'I was going to light a candle.'

'And where's the book? Where is it? Show it to me!'

'I hadn't got it yet. I opened the curtains.'

'And stood admiring yourself. I saw you, parading in your nightclothes. Whom were you expecting?'

'Expecting?'

'Don't try to be clever with me,' Leah said, low and furious. 'You came down here to meet somebody.'

'Leah, I didn't! I came down for a book,'

Beth stammered.

'Is that the truth? Is that the real truth?'

'I came down for a book,' Beth said. 'Truly, Leah. Truly. Whom would I be wanting to meet?'

Leah stared at her for a long moment, and then dropped Beth's wrist and drew her hand across her eyes as if she were trying to rub something out.

'I think you'd better forget about the book and return to your room. Edith is asleep I take it? Or is she roaming about, too?'

'She's asleep. Nothing ever wakes Edith up. Leah, I wasn't going to – I was really coming down to get a book.'

'Then go up to bed and get some sleep. I must go back to the baby.'

'Good night then,' Beth said. Her wrist ached and she felt confused.

'Good night,' Leah said mechanically.

As Beth turned in the archway she saw Leah already reaching up to close out the moonlight.

CHAPTER ELEVEN

The school rose with dignity on the foundations of the old manor house. The architect had carried out Leah's wishes faithfully, the new building occupying the same area as the old building had done, its grey stone blending into the green of trees and lawn. A white ribbon was tied across the front door and Leah stood, scissors in hand, a toque of small yellow rosebuds brightening her sombre grey outfit.

The family stood at one side, a little apart from the group of spectators who had come up from the village to watch the ceremony. All of them had seen the school being built and several of them were hoping to enter their children as pupils. There had been a pleasant buzz of conversation as they agreed among themselves that Miss Leah – begging her pardon Mrs Simmons – had done credit to the Falcons and to Marie Regina. From now on they would be able to hold their heads high, knowing that they too had a school to which their children could be sent.

Miss Leah had even provided a teacher, a cousin of the family who would be coming down from Wales. It was to be hoped that this Mrs Davies could speak the Queen's English, but her being a Falcon kept everything in the family so to speak.

'Ladies and gentlemen.' Leah raised her voice slightly. 'This is a very happy day for me and my family. It gives me great pleasure to declare the Lady Margred School open.'

She snipped the ribbon and there was a polite spattering of applause. Miss Leah, the villagers agreed, might not be the most comfortable of ladies but she had a wonderful sense of occasion.

'Shall we go in?' she invited, and there was pride in her face.

The school was her own personal achievement and for this day at least she could forget the sleepless nights, the suspicions that tore at her, the fear that gripped when she saw Paul smile at Grace or Edith or tease Beth.

A narrow passage divided the large classroom from the cloakroom and kitchen at the other side.

'The children will be given a bowl of hot soup and a sponge pudding at midday,' Leah was explaining as they trooped through. 'We

200

will engage a reliable woman to do the cooking and one of Mrs Stone's girls will be coming up to help. The children can hang their outdoor things up here and leave their overshoes when the weather is bad.'

'You'll be pampering them,' the Vicar said.

'Good food never hurt anyone's learning abilities,' Leah said.

'Of course, of course. Food for the body. Most important.'

Reduced to inferiority, the vicar fell back a little and allowed Leah to continue the tour without interruption.

'We hope to take twenty pupils as a start,' Leah was saying. 'Later there will be more, of course, and then Mrs Davies will require an assistant. The blackboards and slates were sent from London, but the benches are of local wood. Shall we go upstairs?'

A large sitting-room over the schoolroom with an adjoining kitchen and two bedrooms were duly admired. Privately Beth thought the brown carpet and curtains were dull, but she supposed that cousin Wenna would put up her own pictures and ornaments.

'The whole house is perfect,' John was saying. 'I had nothing whatsoever to do with it, so I can give my praise freely. Leah, my dear sister, if Mam were here now, she would be delighted.'

'But she wouldn't,' Beth thought. 'She never believed that children should be sat in rows and made to look at brown curtains. She thought they ought to run freely in the woods, and listen to fairy tales, and take off their shoes to run in the grass.'

'Beth, do pay attention! John was asking if you'd seen Grace,' Leah said.

'Grace? She was with the rest of us a minute ago.'

'Lady Falcon was saying that she didn't feel very well,' Beulah Stone said. 'Mr Simmons offered to take her for a breath of air.'

'And we must be going ourselves,' John said. 'We have a repast laid on up at Kingsmead, ladies and gentlemen, if you would like to follow us. We can provide lifts for those who have no transport in the farm waggons.'

Renewed chattering broke out as they went downstairs. The prospect of not having to face a three-mile walk on a hot afternoon had sent spirits soaring again, and the hospitality of the Falcons was eagerly approved.

'The pony-trap isn't here,' Edith frowned as they came out into the sunshine again.

'Paul must have taken Grace back to the

house,' John said. 'We'll all have to squeeze into the carriage.'

'And make some room for the Vicar,' Beth said mischievously. 'He's far too gouty to climb up on a waggon!'

Edith giggled and Leah shushed her and they stepped up into the carriage holding their bustles and flowered toques and laughing because it was a beautiful day and the opening of the school had finally been accomplished.

Beth, squashed between Edith and the Vicar, chattered as brightly as the rest, ignoring Leah's quelling look, but the feeling that something was wrong, that something dark was going on under the surface, had swept over her again, and she felt a curious reluctance for the drive to end.

The pony-trap was not in the courtyard and Annie, opening the front door as they trooped in, answered John's query with the information that neither Lady Falcon nor Mr Simmons had returned.

'Gone for a breath of air, a spin in the lanes,' the Vicar said heartily.

'No doubt.' But there was a faint crease between Leah's brows as if Beth's mood had touched her.

The long table had been covered with

plates of sandwiches and small cakes. Annie was bringing lemonade for the ladies, and John was persuading the Vicar that the gentlemen ought to have something stronger. Sunlight mellowed the grey stone and there were flowers arranged in a great bowl at the foot of the stairs. Even with a large number of people within it the hall still gave an impression of space, of an emptiness older than the chatter of living things.

Teddy, crowing with pleasure, was being handed about, and admiring comments on his sturdiness were being passed. Leah, excusing herself, had gone upstairs to take off her hat.

'So pleasant to meet like this!' A member of the Sewing Circle cast a longing look at a pink-iced cake, but decided reluctantly against it.

'And such delicious lemonade.' Beulah Stone, whose daughter was to 'help' at the school, sipped appreciatively. It was a pity, she reflected, that the Falcons did not entertain more often. Then everybody would be able to see that despite all the rumours the Falcons were really just like anyone else.

Beth, smiling politely at Mrs Stone, turned and glimpsed Leah coming downstairs again. There was a stiffness in Leah's carriage as if she were holding herself very carefully and, though there was a smile on her lips, her eyes were quite blank as if she were sleepwalking.

'Do have another sandwich, Mrs Whittle.' She was at the foot of the staircase now and her voice was clear, pitched higher than usual but as cold and sweet as the lemonade.

'Grace ought to be here,' John was saying. 'It looks very ill-mannered for the hostess to be absent.'

'I think I can act as hostess with fair efficiency,' Leah said, in the same cold, sweet voice. 'Edith, tell Annie we shall be needing fresh tea. Beth, has the cat stolen your tongue? It is the duty of a young lady to make her guests at ease!'

It was the familiar Leah, and yet a Leah that Beth had never seen before. The elder woman was still moving as if she were asleep, and the smile seemed frozen on her mouth.

Nobody had noticed anything. The food on the table was rapidly diminishing, the last signs of constraint were vanishing in the warmth of conversation. Leah was mingling with the guests, dropping a comment here and there, accepting with a gracious nod of the head the congratulations being offered to her.

'A proud day for you, Mrs Simmons! Marie Regina will, at last, have a school.'

'And meals for the children too! That will be a splendid innovation.'

'No need to send them over to Maidstone.'

'Not that Master Teddy here is going to be concerned with education for several years to come.'

'Such a pretty baby!'

'An intelligent forehead. One can see the breadth of it already.'

Chatter and laughter and the clinking of tea-cups and Leah, smiling and cool, with death in her eyes – Beth could feel the darkness creeping over them all.

'Such a charming occasion,' the Vicar was saying. 'We do appreciate – and I know I speak for all of us – the welcome we have received. Such a pity that Lady Falcon has not – ladies are apt to feel faint on occasions–'

'Grace will be so sorry to have been absent,' Leah smiled.

They were drifting away, shaking hands, thanking John and Leah, smiling at Edith and Beth. The great hall was emptying, the tapestries rustling in the slight breeze from the courtyard as if the building were shaking intruders away. Leah went out to the steps with John to help the less agile ladies up into the waggon. Edith heaved a sigh, announcing to nobody in particular that her feet were killing her. Beth stared down at the brightly hued flowers and saw maggots crawling at their hearts.

'I cannot understand it,' John was saying, 'where can they be.'

'Come into the solar.' Leah came back into the hall, her company smile gone, her voice harsh. 'Come into the solar, all of you!'

'Is anything wrong?' John cast an anxious glance towards the stairs. 'Grace isn't seriously indisposed, is she?'

'Annie will take the baby,' Leah said. 'Come into the solar.'

'Something *is* amiss! Leah, what is it?'

John, followed by his younger sisters, hurried after Leah. The dark-panelled room received them as if it too were waiting for news.

'Grace and Paul have gone,' Leah said flatly. Beth felt sick as if something inside her were rejecting the words.

'Gone where?' Edith asked blankly.

'There was a letter.' Leah brought it out of her reticule and unfolded it in little brisk, angry movements.

'From Grace? A letter from Grace?' John's voice and face were full of confusion.

'She didn't write. Paul did.'

'What does the letter say?' John asked.

'It's very short,' Leah said. 'It says that he and Grace are – in love, as he puts it, and have gone away together. They took the pony trap to the station, I presume, and caught the London train from there. The manuscript is missing and a parcel of Paul's things.'

'He sent Giles to the station with a parcel this morning,' John said slowly. 'I thought it was books.'

'They planned it very cleverly,' Leah said. 'While we were all at the new school, they slipped away.'

'But Grace had nothing with her except a small bag, a little drawstring affair. She wouldn't – is anything of hers missing? Leah, you must be mistaken.'

'I didn't look in your room,' Leah said.

'I'll go up now. This is some terrible misunderstanding.' John went out of the solar and the sound of his hurried footsteps rang back from the stone. The three sisters remained, mute and motionless, their eyes lowered as if each guarded her private thoughts. A bee, trapped behind one of the tiny window panes, buzzed angrily, its feathery wings beating the sun-glinted glass.

The footsteps were returning, heavily and slowly. John, his face working as he held back tears, came into the solar. It was, thought Beth, as if many years had passed and all his youth was fled.

'She has taken her jewels,' he said and in his voice was all the agony of loss.

'We must go after them,' Leah said, and she crumpled the letter into a ball and thrust it deeply into her reticule, as if it were some kind of talisman. 'We must find out where they are.'

'Leah, we cannot! We cannot go after them,' John said. 'We could not compel them to return, and even if they agreed, how could we all continue to live here?'

'I was wrong,' Leah said. 'I was wrong to believe we could marry out of our class. Grace was always vulgar.'

'I love her,' John said. 'I shall always love her, whatever she does.'

'A quiet divorce,' Leah said. Her face was hard and set. 'A quiet divorce will have to be arranged.'

'She is my wife,' John said. 'She was married to me in church. She has borne my child. She will always be my wife.'

'But–' Leah stopped short, pressing her lips tightly together.

'There will be no divorce,' John said, and his voice was firmer than Beth had ever heard it.

'Then I will abide by your decision,' Leah said. 'There will be scandal. It is inevitable. We will have to stand together. We will all have to stand together.'

She was magnificent, Beth thought, gazing at her sister. All the strength of the family had gone into Leah, and even after such a crushing blow she was already gathering up her forces and preparing to resist.

'It's not true,' Edith said suddenly and loudly. 'None of it is true.'

It was the first time she had spoken and the others turned towards her with surprise in their faces, for as she spoke she began to laugh. Her laughter was more shocking than Leah's icy anger or John's resigned despair.

'She's hysterical,' Leah said.

'Hysterical?' Edith controlled herself but went on laughing steadily as if some inner compulsion drove her on. 'It's so funny that you could believe Grace and Paul have run away together! It's so silly because Paul is going to run away with me!'

'Edith, have you lost your senses?' Leah demanded.

'It's true,' Edith said, and her laughter stopped as abruptly as if it had been cut with a knife. 'Paul and I have been lovers for months. He always liked me more than he liked you. He married you for your money, but he loved me. He loved me and I'm going to have his baby.'

'Edith, for the love of God!' John interrupted. 'Beth, you ought not to be hearing such shocking things.'

Beth could not have moved even if she had wished it. Her legs were shaking violently and she gripped the edge of a chair so tightly that her palm was numb.

'Next March. End of March or beginning of April,' Edith said. 'We had planned to go away together, I would have been free of Kingsmead, free of you all! We used to meet down in the cottage, when you were busy at the school or at some Sewing Club meeting. We used to meet there and laugh at you. We laughed at you, Leah! And we made love, Leah! Over and over again we made love, Leah!'

She broke off with a cry of pain as Leah

211

slapped her viciously across the face.

'We must be calm,' John implored. 'We must stand together. You said that we must all stand together, Leah.'

'Why not?' Leah's voice was light. Only her eyes blazed in her colourless face. 'Why not stand together? After all, you and I are in the same condition, my dear Edith. I too am to have a child next March.'

'That's not possible,' Edith whispered. 'Paul said–'

'That he and I no longer – that we were not living as husband and wife? He lied about that. He lied about many things. I am going to have his child.'

'But he promised that we were going away together.' Edith sat down on the sofa and began to cry. 'He said we could go to Paris. I come into my money soon. We were going to live in Paris. He promised me!'

'It seems that he chose Grace and her jewels,' Leah said.

John too had sat down and his face was haggard as he looked up at his sister and asked,

'What's to be done? What can any of us do?'

'Hush! Let me think,' Leah spoke calmly, all the hurt locked away from her expression.

'There will be no hiding the fact that the two of them went away together. Somebody will have seen them getting on the train, if they went by train, but I'm certain they did. We can only hope that good-taste and respect will cut short any – gossip. And there's Edith. The disgrace would be – it is not to be contemplated.'

'You need not consider me,' Edith sobbed. 'After all, you've never considered me before.'

'I am considering the reputation of the family,' Leah said, 'Grace and Paul...' she hesitated and her face twitched violently, and then was calm again. 'What they have done is quite horrible, unspeakably so, but it's no reflection on us. It's no reflection on our characters. But for Edith to disgrace the family – let me think! We are both with child. Both with– Edith, you will have to go away for a visit. You will have to go away for a long visit.'

'The child could be adopted. Is that what you're saying, Leah?' John asked.

'The child is a Falcon,' Leah said. 'Whatever its beginnings the child is a Falcon, part of the family.'

'I will not pretend to be a widow,' Edith sobbed.

'You're so stupid!' Leah cried. 'You are so unutterably stupid! I will have two babies, that's all.'

'Two?' John looked at her.

'Twins have occurred several times in the family. There is nothing so unusual about twins after all. And I shall have twins, legitimately born but deserted by their father before the event. The shame will be somewhat mitigated.'

'Oh, no!' Edith leapt to her feet, her tear-stained face crimson. 'You'll not have my child as you have Teddy! I've seen the way you wheedled him out of his mother's arms, making him love you more than her. You'll not get my child too!'

'It would be a solution,' John pleaded.

'She won't get my baby!' Edith shrilled. 'She took the man I wanted, but she'll not have my child too. And I'm not going to run away and hide either. I'm going to stay right here and have it!'

'You will leave Kingsmead tonight,' Leah said. 'You will pack a bag and leave tonight.'

'You seem to forget,' Edith retorted, 'that this is not your house. It's John's house, and only he has the right to turn me out of it.'

'You've always said you wanted to leave the village and travel to London,' John said.

214

'I've changed my mind,' Edith said and sat down again, folding her lips in a stubborn line.

'You can go and stay at Witch's Dower if you like,' Beth said.

'In that poky little place! No, thank you,' Edith snapped.

'You can't stay at Kingsmead,' Leah said flatly.

'There'd not be one moment's contentment for either of you,' John said wearily.

'I'll go and live at Whittle Farm,' Edith said suddenly. 'It's been empty for months. I'll go and live there.'

Beth stared at her in astonishment. The farm at the other side of the old monastery ruins had been in the Falcon family since the late seventeenth century but had been either rented out or occupied by various bailiffs. The idea of Edith living there was ludicrous.

'Whittle Farm belongs to John, too. He'll not have you there,' Leah said.

'Then I'll stand up in the church and ask if somebody in the village can provide a home for an unmarried woman and her bastard child!' Edith shrilled.

'Perhaps it would be as well if Edith moved to the farm,' John said. 'The house is

215

in an excellent condition and I'm sure two girls from the village could be employed as servants.'

'You'd allow her to flaunt her shame on your property?' Leah threw up her hands in despair.

'It's all our shame,' John said and Beth, listening, thought she had never heard her brother sound so firm. 'Edith should have been allowed to wed long ago. I should have taken her to London and escorted her to parties and balls. We have stayed too quietly here since Mam died. I blame myself.'

'Dear John, it's not your fault,' Edith said, beginning to cry again. 'I never wanted to bring shame upon you!'

'She is glad enough to shame me,' Leah said bitterly. Beth slipped away, her own heart too heavy for tears. In a brief afternoon all the security of her childhood had vanished. The world of Kingsmead had been torn apart, and a new world had intruded, a world in which husbands deserted their wives and seduced their sisters-in-law. A world in which sisters could hate and children born out of an act of love were called bastards and despised.

She could no longer bear to stay in the house and feel the waves of hatred and sorrow flowing into the grey walls. The others must settle what was to be done, but for a little while she needed to be out of the house, out in the green meadows where the afternoon shadows had grown long and the evening blossoms were beginning to fold.

She began to run, her long tail of hair bumping against her back. When she reached the woods she slowed her steps and began to cry, her breath coming in little sobbing gasps, the tears streaking her cheeks.

In a way she was crying for all of them, for they had all lost something; John his wife, Leah her husband, Edith her lover, Teddy his mother.

'And I,' thought Beth, 'have lost nothing at all, because I have never had anyone to lose except Papa and Mama.'

Edith had been Papa's special girl, but Mam and Beth had been closer even than those two, for both bore upon their thighs the purple crescent that was the outward sign of inward power.

'Folk smile in the city at talk of witches,' Mam had said, 'but country people have more sense. They know there are veils to be lifted and secrets to be revealed to those who know how to keep them or use them.'

Mam had never lost the soft upward inflections of her Welsh accent, and her amber eyes had glowed softly as if the secrets she held were precious.

But after Papa's death the yellow eyes had grown dull and Mama had stopped brushing her hair and crept about with a lost bewildered expression on her face, until she had begun to smile again and tilt her head as if she were listening for something.

'I wish you were here now,' Beth said aloud. 'Oh, Mam, I wish you hadn't died!'

Only the rustling of the trees answered her. She threaded her way between them and came into the clearing. The little house waited for her as it always waited. She supposed that Paul had met Edith here, and probably Grace too, but it made no difference for the cottage, in its time, must have sheltered many lovers. Beth went into the living-room and sat down. It was cool and dim and peaceful here, and she began to cry all over again, the tears sliding down her cheeks and splashing on her fingers. This time she was crying only for herself.

CHAPTER TWELVE

There had not been so much excitement in Marie Regina since the night they had carried Lord Harry home with a broken neck. In a way this event was worse. It had been possible to offer sympathy to the family then, but it was unthinkable to offer condolences to Lord John and Miss Leah because their respective mates had run away together.

'Bold as brass together at the station!'

'Sam Gibbs saw them getting on the London train.'

'They even asked him to make sure that somebody drove back the pony-trap to Kingsmead!'

'They must have been carrying on under the noses of the whole family.'

'And poor little Teddy Falcon left without a mother!'

'Not that she was ever much of a mother. Miss Leah has been like a mother to that child since he was born.'

'And Miss Edith packing up and moving

into Whittle Farm the very next day. It's my belief that she stood up for the pair of them and Miss Leah lost her temper.'

Rumour and counter rumour wove its web of gossip.

Beth, waiting with John on the platform, was aware of the covert glances of those who passed by. John himself had made only one brief, sad comment.

'The last time I came here was to meet Leah – and Grace.'

Beth squeezed his hand wishing she could comfort him, but he drew away slightly, forcing a smile as the distant whistle of the train heralded its approach.

A few moments later they were greeting a slim brown-haired girl with sleepy green eyes who stepped from the carriage, pulling a large canvas bag after her.

'Cousin Wenna? May we call you that, my dear, for you are one of the family though we have never met before. I am John Falcon and this is my sister, Beth. We are going straight to the school, so that you can settle in, and tomorrow we will bring you over to Kingsmead. My other sister, Leah, will receive you then. She has not been very well these past few days and asks to be excused for her bad manners.'

John was shaking hands and taking the canvas bag. Beth, shaking hands in her turn, looked up into a round, smooth face in which only the heavy lidded eyes were unusual.

'Cousin John. Cousin Beth.' Wenna had an odd, husky voice that came out in short gasps as if she had been running. 'It's very good to be here. Such a long way it is!'

'And your mother is well?' John asked, helping her up into the trap.

'Helping,' thought Beth, was perhaps not the right word, for Wenna sprang up as lightly as a boy.

'She never ails,' the young woman assured him. 'Up with the chickens and to bed with the chickens. Up to her ankles in cow dung half the day.'

John chuckled. It was the first time that Beth had heard him laugh since Grace had gone. She felt a rush of gratitude towards her cousin.

They drove the long way round, down the main road, passing the gates of Kingsmead and the bridle path that dipped down towards the cottage, rattling over the wooden bridge. Wenna, glancing to the right where the graveyard sloped down into the village, said in her breathless way,

'So many headstones!'

'I fear we are so used to them that they no longer affect us as they should,' John apologized.

'Oh, I like graveyards,' Wenna said cheerfully. 'And funerals. There's nothing like a good funeral. My husband had a lovely one.'

'We have not yet condoled with you on your sad loss,' John said.

'Yes, it was very sad at the time,' Wenna said with undiminished cheerfulness, 'but he was a good Chapel man and probably went straight to heaven, so no sense in grieving, is there?'

John, turning the pony trap into the drive that led to the school, chuckled again.

Within a few minutes the school itself came into view, and Maggie Stone, who had been peeping out of the front window, opened the front door.

'My sister, Leah, will tell you about the pupils you can expect,' John said as they mounted the stairs. 'I leave all that part of it to her. These are your rooms. I hope you'll not be nervous sleeping here alone.'

'I'm never nervous,' Wenna said tranquilly. 'I'd like a dog though. It will be all right if I buy a dog?'

'You may buy a dozen. This is your home and you must do as you please in it.' John put down her canvas bag. 'We have foxhounds, but they are kept for hunting. Leah won't have them near the house. She is not fond of animals.'

'I like them,' Wenna said briefly 'Some of them have more sense than people. Is this house haunted?'

'My dear cousin, of course not,' John gave her an astonished look. 'Even if one believed in such superstition, this is a new building and hardly likely to be affected.'

'It's the place, not the building.' Wenna took off her hat. 'Not that I mind ghosts. Leave them alone and they'll leave you alone, I say. But it's more comfortable without them. When am I supposed to begin teaching school?'

'Leah thinks that next week will be soon enough to begin,' John said. 'You will want to find your way around, perhaps go over to Maidstone. There are two docile ponies in the stable. You do ride?'

'Anything on four legs,' Wenna assured him. 'I think I'll make myself a cup of tea. Will you stay and drink it with me?'

'Beth will stay. I must let Leah know that you arrived safely. There is plenty of food in the kitchen.'

'Another time then.' She shook hands cordially. 'Will you walk back, or shall I leave you the trap?' John enquired of his sister.

'I'll walk,' Beth said promptly.

Cousin Wenna fascinated her. The dowdy jacket and skirt, the tightly coiled hair, were so at variance with the sleepy green eyes and husky voice.

'Tell me about everybody,' Wenna invited when John had taken his departure. 'I'll make the tea and find out what's in the larder, and you can talk. There's something wrong here, isn't there?'

'Wrong?' Beth asked.

'Your brother looks unhappy, and your sister didn't come to meet me. Is she regretting asking me to teach here? I'd not be surprised or offended, for I've never taught school in my life.'

'We have had some – trouble here,' Beth hesitated.

'Oh?' Spoon poised over the caddy, Wenna stared at her.

'Leah's husband and John's wife – they ran away together. Leah is with child, so she was naturally angry.'

'Why naturally?' Wenna enquired. 'She

didn't own her husband, did she? But it wasn't a very polite thing for him to do. In a small place there's bound to be talk. There was over my Aunt Saran, so I've been told.'

'Who was Aunt Saran?' Beth watched as the older girl kindled the fire and put on the kettle.

'She was your grandmother. Did your own mother never speak of her?'

'Mam never talked much of her child-hood,' Beth said.

'Afraid her grand English cousins would be ashamed,' Wenna said tolerantly. 'But there's always been a strain of Welsh blood in the Falcons. There was Mair Falcon who ran away from her husband and went back to her old home in Wales. She had twins after she went back to the farm. One was my mother Catrin and the other was Saran.'

'Mam's mother?'

'Pretty as an April day she was,' Wenna said, cutting bread energetically. 'She was seduced by a travelling tinker one afternoon and died when your mother was born.'

'Are you saying Mam was a–!' Beth stared at her in astonishment.

'My own mother reared her until she was of an age to fend for herself, and then down she came into Kent to seek out her English relatives. The next my mother heard was that she'd wed her cousin, Lord Harry. His own wife and stepmother had just been killed.'

'By lightning. I know about that.'

'And seven months after the wedding your sister Leah was born. Just under the fence in time, as we say. Shall we have gooseberry preserve?'

'Are you saying that Leah was conceived – out of wedlock?'

'Oh, I should think so. Most folk are. I'll just call down and tell that little girl that opened the door that she can go home. I suppose I'll have to get used to being waited on now. You can brew the tea if you will.'

Wenna went briskly out, leaving Beth in a state of horrified fascination. That Leah, of all people, had been almost a bastard! That Mama and Papa had – Beth closed her eyes in an attempt to collect her senses.

'I'll carry everything in. I'm used to hard work.' Wenna had returned and was piling up a tray.

'I'm sure that Leah doesn't know,' Beth said, trotting after her.

'She probably never troubled to count up,' Wenna said. 'It's not important anyway. Being unwed doesn't stop you having babies, and being wed doesn't stop husbands and wives running off. It's the loving that matters. What about the rest of my cousins? Isn't there a sister – Edith?'

'Edith is living at Whittle Farm. That's a property we own at the other side of the ruins.'

'All this property! I'd never be able to keep track of it.' Wenna shook her head and passed the scones. 'Is cousin Edith married?'

'N-not exactly.'

'You mean she has a man.'

'No, not exactly that either, but she's – there's going to be a baby, only nobody knows yet except the family. Of course everybody in Marie Regina will find out soon.'

'Then it's brave of her to stay here.'

'I think,' said Beth, impelled to honesty, 'that she stayed to spite Leah. Leah was very shocked when she found out what had happened.'

'Who was the father?' Wenna asked.

Beth hesitated. Cousin Wenna might be one of the family, but Leah was already shamed by being deserted. No need to shame her further.

'Edith won't tell,' she said at last.

'These travelling men!' Wenna's green eyes

twinkled. 'Well, your sister has a right to be silent. But all this must have happened very recently, since Cousin Leah offered me the school?'

'All at once,' Beth said. 'Everything happened all at once. Paul and Grace ran away together, and Leah quarrelled with Edith.'

'It must have been very interesting,' Wenna said, reducing the dramatic implications with her matter-of-fact tone. 'Life is very interesting, I've found. One can go on quietly for years and then the whole world explodes. Sometimes I think it would be marvellous to live for ever, don't you?'

'I'm not sure,' Beth said, bemused by this extraordinary newcomer.

'I will go over to see your sister Edith,' Wenna said. 'And isn't there a brother too, apart from Cousin John?'

'Price,' Beth nodded. 'Price went out to South Africa to look for diamonds. We've had a couple of short letters from him, but we're not much of a family for writing letters. He will probably come back one day, loaded with jewels. Grace took all hers with her.'

'Cousin John's wife? But won't he divorce her now?' 'There's never been a divorce in the family,' Beth said. 'It would be very shocking!'

'Not as shocking as staying married when there's no love left,' Wenna said calmly. 'Have you had sufficient tea?'

'And I have to go home.'

'To report on me to Leah?' The green eyes gleamed with amusement. 'Why, surely John will have done that already?'

'I have to give up the keys.' Embarrassed, Beth fished for them. 'Are you certain you'll be all right?'

'I'll unpack my bits and pieces, and wander round my school,' Wenna said.

She had, Beth noticed, already established herself as mistress of her domain.

'I do hope you'll be happy here,' Beth said.

'I generally contrive to be happy,' Wenna said, 'and I've looked forward to coming here. I've often wondered what my Falcon cousins were like. But you've told me nothing about yourself. Don't you have a lover or a gentleman caller? How old are you?'

'Eighteen – nineteen next March. And I don't have any gentlemen callers.'

'You ought to have. You are a very pretty young woman.'

'One day,' Beth said vaguely, and shook

hands again as she left.

Wenna watched the small figure go down the stairs and was conscious, after the front door closed, of the empty silence. This building was like a shell. It needed to be filled with voices and footsteps and laughter. She rather thought she would enjoy teaching children. Her own education had been limited, for her mother never mingled with the neighbours nor sent her daughter to any local school, but Wenna, having learned to read, write, and cipher, had devoured every book she could find.

It would be interesting to teach children. She imagined rows of them with shining faces and starched pinafores, eagerly drinking in whatever she chose to say. She would have liked a child of her own but the death of her husband in the quarry had ended her hopes. For a time at least, she mentally corrected herself, for there was always the possibility that she might marry again.

In the solar at Kingsmead Leah sat in her usual place on the window-seat. She had resumed her black dress and above its high collar her face was sharp and white.

'So Cousin Wenna is a pleasant young lady? I shall be interested in meeting her tomorrow. You saw she had everything she needed, Beth?'

'We had some tea together,' Beth said. 'I told her all about the family.'

'All?' Leah raised her brows.

'Not quite all,' Beth said hastily. 'She doesn't know Paul is the father of the baby that Edith is going to have.'

'Am I to understand that you babbled about everything else?'

'You said Cousin Wenna was a member of the family,' Beth protested. 'You offered her the school because of it.'

'She wished to have a change of scene,' Leah said coldly. 'It seemed an opportunity for the school to acquire a teacher, but initially for a probationary period. There is no need to tell them all our private business.'

'But she will find out sooner or later. Everybody will,' Beth argued.

'But nobody must know that Paul and Edith – John, Edith gave you her promise on that, didn't she?'

'The father of the child will remain unknown,' John said wearily.

'There will be no further scandal when Edith's condition becomes apparent, but to have it known that Paul – that would be the ultimate disgrace,' Leah said.

231

Beth, watching the still, white face, listening to the cold, steady voice, wondered if Leah ever wept for the husband who had deserted her. It seemed that she did not, for her eyes were dry and clear as if she slept soundly every night. In contrast John looked tired and grey, but he had been more like his old self when they had been with cousin Wenna.

'I think Wenna will be discreet,' John said. 'She struck me as a very sensible young woman, quite refreshingly frank. You will like her, Leah.'

'Let us hope so. Unfortunately neither you nor I are very good judges of character,' Leah said dryly. 'I must go up to Teddy. He was a mite feverish earlier.'

She rose and went unhurriedly from the room. John looked across at Beth and made a bitter little grimace.

'Leah is right,' he said wryly. 'We are not good at judging character, we Falcons. I would not have dreamed that Grace – well, it's no matter now. We cannot turn back the clock. And I have the child. Teddy means a very great deal to me.'

He sighed more like an old man than a young one, and followed his sister out of the room.

After a while Beth rose and went through the hall into the courtyard. The moon was rising and the old feeling of restlessness had swelled up in her.

Outside it was cool and dark, with the great house a lighted blur behind her. She wandered beneath the arch and down the drive, wishing she dare go to Witch's Dower. She would have liked to spend a night in the little house, but Leah would be horrified at the idea. Both Leah and John still treated her as if she were a small child, but there were many times when she felt immeasurably old and sad.

The moon had risen higher and its light turned the road to silver. Beth leaned against the main gates and turned her face up to the horned crescent. The trotting of hoofs down the road was like the beating of her heart.

The horse was slowing, its stride lengthening from trot to walk. A man whose face was darkness under a broad brimmed hat leaned to speak to her.

'Are you real, young lady, or a nymph turned into a statue?'

'I'm real,' Beth said blankly.

'And able to give me directions, I hope? I am bound for Maidstone. Is this still the right road?'

'You came on horseback from–?'

'From London. I'm not one of those people who enjoy travelling in stuffy carriages.'

'You'll not get to Maidstone tonight,' Beth said. 'There's an inn down in the village.'

'I dislike inns,' the stranger said. 'If I get too weary I will simply roll myself up in my blanket, use my saddle as a pillow and sleep.'

'Are you a travelling man?' Beth enquired suspiciously.

'I'm an artist. Do I look like a – what was it? – a travelling man?'

'I've never seen one,' Beth confessed, 'but I'm told they have very bad habits.'

'Do they indeed?' The man's light, pleasant laugh rang out. 'Then allow me to reassure, or disappoint you. My name is Michael Shaw and I'm a very respectable artist with very good habits.'

'I'm Elizabeth Falcon.' She reached up to shake hands. 'People call me Beth. Why do you want to sleep in the open?'

'Because, having had a bad attack of bronchitis my doctor advised open air, countryside, and leisure.'

'But sleeping in the open isn't going to do

your bronchitis much good,' Beth said. 'Now, if you really want a place to sleep, the inn is very comfortable.'

'And I am temporarily out of funds.'

'Oh.' She looked at him wishing she could see his face properly, but it was shaded by his hat and the heavy travelling cloak he wore was highly collared.

'Maidstone is the next town marked on the map I have. Best if I make for there,' he said.

'Wait.' Beth caught at his rein. 'I have a cottage.'

'Of course. In every fairy-tale there is a beautiful girl who lives in a cottage.'

'I don't live in it. I live at Kingsmead with my family, but there is a cottage and it does belong to me. If you follow the road, just before you come to the bridge there is a steep path on the left leading into the trees. If you follow it you'll come to the cottage. You can sleep there if you like. The door isn't locked and there is clean linen. I light a fire in the place two or three times a week so everything will be aired.'

'My dear Miss er-Beth, I cannot walk into a completely strange house at your invitation,' the man said.

'I thought artists didn't mind about the

conventions,' Beth said.

'I am only a part-time artist,' Michael Shaw said wryly. 'I work in a bank for a living and confine my artistic pursuits to high days and holidays. This is a month's leave-of-absence, for health reasons and because my employer is an unusually generous man. So I hired a horse, packed up my palette, and set off.'

'Without any money?'

'I have some, but not enough to squander on inns. I was hoping to rent somewhere cheaply in Maidstone.'

'Oh, I see.'

Beth, who had never had to worry about money or the shortage of it, bit her lip.

'Why are you going to Maidstone anyway?' she enquired. 'I thought people went on painting holidays to France or somewhere like that.'

'Have you never heard that Kent is the garden of England?' he returned. 'We are too fond of rushing across to other countries and never take a good look at the beauties of our own. To put that beauty on canvas for other people to enjoy is not such a bad thing, is it?'

'I think it would be wonderful,' Beth said with enthusiasm. 'But the cottage – why, you could stay there for a while if you chose. It's my property and I can do with it what I choose. At least think about it, Mr Shaw.'

It was suddenly very important that he should agree to stay, as if in riding out of the night towards her he had brought something new and hopeful into her life.

'You're a very persuasive young woman.' She caught the gleam of white teeth in the dark-angled face. 'I'm almost minded to take advantage of your kind offer.'

'It's the path on the left just before the bridge,' she said. 'And you're welcome to make use of the place.'

He sketched a salute and rode on, his cloaked figure and slouched hat becoming a part of the landscape again. She watched him go, listened to the receding hoofbeats, and felt the restlessness again stronger than before.

'Beth! Beth, what in the world are you doing out here?' Leah, sounding annoyed, was coming down the drive, her heels tapping sharply.

'I was looking at the moon,' Beth said.

'And talking to it as well from what I heard!'

'Oh, not to the moon. I was talking to a gentleman.'

'What gentleman?' Leah demanded.

'His name is Michael Shaw. He was looking for lodgings, so I said he could stay at Witch's Dower.'

'You said what!'

'I said he could stay at Witch's Dower.'

'You invited a complete stranger to walk into the cottage in the middle of the night! Beth, have you completely lost your senses?'

'It's my property,' Beth said sulkily. 'He's a most respectable gentleman.'

'How can you possibly know that? What does he do?'

'He's on a painting holiday,' Beth said defensively, 'but he works in a bank though he doesn't like stuffy inns. And he wants to paint pictures of Kent for other folk to enjoy because it's the garden of England and too many people rush abroad these days.'

'He seems to have told you a great deal about himself,' Leah said wryly. 'I suppose you chatted as freely to him.'

'I told him my name and said that he could stay in the cottage,' Beth said.

'Then someone will have to go down and tell him that he cannot stay, that's all.'

'It belongs to me,' Beth said, a kind of panic rising up in her. 'Witch's Dower is mine. Mam left it to me, and I have the right to let anyone I please stay there. I don't want you to spoil it, Leah.'

'I'll talk to John,' Leah said, and turned back towards the house.

Beth took one last, imploring look at the moon and followed.

CHAPTER THIRTEEN

'He may not be here at all,' Beth said, as she and John rode down the bridle path. 'He didn't actually accept my offer.'

'Leah was right. You should not have talked to a complete stranger,' John scolded.

'But if he's there you promised–'

'That I'd talk to him and ascertain his honesty and respectability. I've promised nothing more.'

'He is there!' Beth interrupted. 'He's painting the cottage.'

Michael Shaw, his back to them, was sitting on a stool in front of an easel on which a canvas was propped.

At the sound of their approach he turned, brush and palette in his hands.

He was older than Beth had imagined, the

black hair winged with grey, his face lean and dark with deep lines of frustration scored on brow and cheeks.

'Mr Shaw?' John dismounted and went forward with outstretched hand. 'My sister has told me about you. I am Lord Falcon. John Falcon.'

'Excuse me for not shaking hands. I'm covered in smudges.'

Michael Shaw bowed, apparently un-embarrassed by the encounter. It was the younger man who flushed as he said,

'My sister acted in a very forward manner last evening. I'm afraid you must have thought it somewhat eccentric.'

'I thought it most charming of her to offer hospitality so spontaneously,' Michael Shaw said, 'but I wasn't certain if I ought to accept. I am relieved to have the opportunity of meeting you. Of course, I intend to pay adequate rent for the three weeks I'll be here.'

'Three weeks? You said a month!' Beth said in disappointment.

'I have to allow myself a few days at home in order to get the work I've done varnished.'

'Home?' John queried.

'London. I have a card somewhere.'

240

'There really is no need, sir.' John had flushed again.

'There is every need.' Michael Shaw had a tinge of amusement in his voice. 'If my sister invited a stranger to lodge I would certainly wish to know about him. She may have told you that I work in a bank. It's not the most romantic of occupations, but–'

'My dear sir, there is really no need at all,' John protested. 'It was simply that my sister Leah was a little worried. Beth is apt to be impulsive.'

'I can understand your concern,' Michael Shaw said. 'My bank, Nicholson's can provide adequate references if you care to apply: As to rent–'

'You must have a talk with Beth about that,' John said. 'Witch's Dower is her property.'

'Is that the name of the cottage? Obviously there's a story attached to it.'

'Which my sister will only be too pleased to relate to you. I'm going over to the school, Beth, to see if Cousin Wenna has settled in and has everything she needs. Good-day, sir.'

He remounted and rode out of the clearing, his air of relief betraying his distaste for the interview.

241

'Your brother is very young,' Michael Shaw said, 'and very conscious of his responsibilities.'

'He seems quite old to me,' Beth said. 'He's very proper, you know. He and my sister Leah take their duties very much to heart.'

'I am forty-five,' Michael Shaw said, 'and anyone younger than that seems very young indeed to me.'

'You don't look so old,' she said kindly. 'I'm nineteen – well, almost, and that can feel very old sometimes.'

'You are no age at all,' he bowed gallantly. 'By moonlight you are as old as Hecate and in the sunshine you are Diana. Why "Witch's Dower"?'

'Some of my ancestors were witches,' she explained. 'They were not all bad ones, you know, but one of them was drowned by the villagers hundreds of years ago.'

'And no doubt walks the cottage.'

'Nothing walks in the cottage,' she said laughing. 'They are all quiet in their graves these days.'

'I'm happy to hear it,' he said solemnly. 'We were going to discuss rent, I think?'

'I was just wondering,' Beth said shyly, 'if, instead of real rent, you could let me have a picture of the cottage.'

'I am only an amateur,' he warned.

'But you've already begun one.' She indicated the canvas.

'It's an interesting house,' he said. 'I hoped you wouldn't mind my painting it, but as rent – no, you must accept more.'

'Could you paint me?' she ventured. 'It would be very flattering for me to remember when I'm an old lady.'

'To remember that a bank-clerk on holiday painted your portrait?'

There was a bitterness in his face that was beyond her understanding but she put her hand on his arm and said,

'I would remember that an artist rode into Marie Regina and was kind enough to stay.'

'You're a *kind* child,' he said, and his smile was warm. 'Would you like to come into your own property? I took the liberty of brewing some tea this morning. There was some in the cupboard.'

'But no milk.' She looked at him in concern as they passed beneath the lintel. 'You will have to get supplies in from the village.'

'I intend to explore later. As you can see, nothing has been disturbed.'

'You're very neat. I thought all artists were untidy.'

'But I'm not a real artist. I've sold half a dozen small canvasses in my entire life. Would you like some black tea?'

She shook her head, wanting to stay, wanting to go on talking to him. It was strange for they had only just met, but she felt they had known each other for years and that there were no constraints between them.

'I haven't meddled with anything,' he said, 'but I couldn't help noticing the room on the right. It looks as if it were intended to be a kitchen, but some of the contents of the jars would surely make strange soups!'

'It's the herb-room,' Beth told him.

'Where the witches used to stir their cauldrons? And now the house is yours.'

'It's not part of the main estate,' she explained. 'My mother left it to me when she died.'

'And you, in turn, will leave it to your own daughter.'

'If I ever have one.' She was silent for a moment and the man, looking at her, saw that her eyes had a queer dazed look, but a moment later she was smiling again, chattering lightly about her sister Leah, and a cousin who had come down from Wales to teach in the school built on Falcon land.

She was, he thought, an enchanting creature, just growing into womanhood but not completely awakened. There was a faint dusting of freckles on her nose and her ankles, beneath the short riding skirt, were slender. A tenderness that hovered on the edge of desire leapt up in him.

'But you haven't told me about yourself,' she was saying.

'It's a dull story. I was born, went into banking, and took a holiday in Kent. My wife thinks I'm crazy to pack a folding easel and hire a horse instead of travelling in comfort to Brighton where I could look round the shops. Susan's idea of heaven is looking round the shops.'

'Wife?'

'My wife's name is Susan.'

'I see.' Beth fiddled with the lacing on her jacket and asked brightly, 'I suppose you've been married a long time?'

'Twenty years.'

'And you have children?'

'Susan never cared for children,' he said briefly. 'She enjoys her home and the company of her friends.'

'And looking round shops.'

'That too.' He smiled again. 'But all ladies like looking at shops, don't they?'

'Not me,' Beth said with decision. 'I go to Maidstone sometimes, but looking at things in shops is very boring. Except for china and books. I like beautiful, thin china and fat books that smell of all the people that ever read them.'

'What else do you like?' He had taken a piece of charcoal and was making swift, blurred strokes with it on a pad.

'I like rivers,' she said dreamily, 'and the songs Mam used to sing, and pretty dresses, and the moonlight shining through the leaves of the trees and – oh, many things.'

'The moon is your planet,' he told her.

'I have a moonstone.' She held out her hand on the middle finger of which a milky stone shimmered with blue and green lights. 'Mam left each of us a ring when she died. Leah has the diamond, and Edith the pearl and I have the moonstone. It's not an expensive ring, but I like it.'

'It suits your hand. Keep your head still.'

'Are you drawing me?'

'A preliminary sketch. I'll develop it later.'

'Shall I stop talking?' she enquired anxiously. 'Leah tells me I chatter too much.'

'Chatter as much as you please,' he said absently, but she held her peace, seeing that part of him had forgotten her as a person and regarded her as an arrangement of curves and lines to be translated onto paper.

'It's not good,' he said at last, 'but the light is bad.'

She looked at her own face, its contours not completely defined, the eyes dreaming.

'It's good,' she said at last. 'It's very good. Your wife – she must be very proud of you.'

'Must she?' He took back the drawing and looking at it said. 'We have not lived as man and wife for years. I want you to know that.'

'I'm – sorry.' She was aware that such matters ought not to be mentioned between the sexes, that she ought to be shocked at his talking of such things, but she felt only sadness as if all the wasted years cried out in his voice.

'We rub along,' he said, 'without love and without hatred. We are held together by a vast indifference. I've never spoken of this to anybody before. God knows why I'm telling you.'

'Because this is your holiday,' she said, with a wisdom beyond her years. 'In three weeks you will go away and we may never meet again. So you can talk freely.'

'We may never part,' he said, and the sentence hung like a warning in the air.

'You know what I think,' Beth said, abruptly and feverishly gay. 'I think we should ride into the village and buy some food and have a picnic on the hill.'

'Wouldn't your family object?'

'Not they! John will be taking Wenna over to see my sister Leah, and he will tell them all that you are a respectable elderly gentleman in whose care I shall be very safe. You can sketch upon the hill. The ruins are very picturesque.'

'Then, by all means,' he bowed, 'let us go and see these picturesque ruins.'

'And buy some food,' she reminded him. 'You must be hungry.'

'Yes,' he said, and something in his face made her begin to chatter again very fast.

Edith, standing in the yard of Whittle Farm, looked up and saw, far off amid the grey walls and crumbling arches of the old monastery, two figures. They were too far away for her to make them out clearly and after a few moments she turned and went back into the house.

Whittle Farm was a small manor house, retaining many of its original features. A Whittle woman had once married the brother of a Falcon wife and the property itself, through a combination of events, had become part of the main estate.

The house was simply designed with two small parlours and a large, low-ceilinged kitchen. There were three bedrooms above and while the whole might have sufficed a large Tudor family, Edith found it cramped and confining. It was comfortably but not luxuriously furnished, and John had brought over his sister's possessions. He had also engaged two girls to do the cleaning and cooking, and promised that he would continue to see that the land was farmed.

She sat dolefully by the fire, her chin propped on her hand. She was aware that by leaving Kingsmead she had helped to inflame the gossip in the village, it being generally agreed that she and Leah must have quarrelled about the elopement of Grace and Paul. Well, there would be more gossip when her condition became obvious. She wished that she could let everybody know how Leah had been doubly shamed, but John had begged her to say nothing about the father of her child, and out of compassion for his own loss she had promised to remain silent.

Of her own disgrace she did not think very much. Paul Simmons had pretended to love her and had deserted her knowing she was to bear his child. In a way that was worse than his desertion of Leah for he had not known of her condition.

'I really did love him,' she whispered aloud. 'I really did.'

The contemplation of her own heartbreak was so intense that it induced a fit of hopeless weeping. The two servants were in the kitchen but she was past caring if they heard her.

When she had cried for a long time she rose and went over to the writing-desk. At least she could pour out her feelings to her favourite brother and let him know how badly she had been treated. Her handwriting scrawled untidily across the sheet.

Dear Price,

You will be surprised to see from the address that I have moved to Whittle Farm. We have had so much trouble that I scarcely know where to begin. Paul has betrayed us all most shamefully, for he has led me to believe that he loved me and coaxed me into doing great wrong for which I am very sorry, but none of it would have happened if Leah would have allowed me to have a husband. But I am with child by him and Leah will not have me at Kingsmead any longer. But that is not the worst of it, my dear brother, for Paul has eloped with John's wife, Grace. I never understood how John could come to marry such a vulgar, red-haired actress and with a surname like Finn too! But it is all too shocking and there is nobody to whom I can talk.

Her pen pushed on, the words tumbling out, her tears dried on her cheeks and her head ached more fiercely than her heart.

At Kingsmead, later that day, Leah sat with Teddy on her knee and pronounced judgment on Cousin Wenna who had just ridden back to the school.

'She seems pleasant and intelligent, though her manner of speaking is perhaps a little free, but she has had very few advantages so we must make some allowances.'

'She struck me as refreshing,' John said. 'Your idea of asking her to run the school, was an excellent one. And the salary pleased her, I think.'

'I should hope so. Two hundred pounds a year is more than adequate,' Leah said, joggling the baby who crowed and clutched at her.

'And Cousin Wenna will work very hard if my impressions are correct,' John said.

'One hopes so. I wish I could feel as content in my mind about Beth,' Leah said.

'Beth is all right, isn't she?' John gave the other a surprised glance. 'I thought she took the recent upheaval very well.'

'She was not directly involved,' Leah said sharply. 'Beth is still a child in many ways, but she is impulsive.'

'It seems to be a family failing,' John said with bitter humour.

'She is more impulsive than any of us,' Leah frowned. 'Both you and I have been cruelly mistaken in our estimation of character, but neither of us has ever rushed out into the moonlight and invited a perfect stranger to become a lodger.'

'Only for three weeks,' John said, 'and he is a very respectable gentleman. His manner impressed me most favourably. Most favourably indeed.'

'But to allow them to ride off alone together to a picnic!'

'They were buying some provisions in the village. It was quite innocent, Leah, and he is so much older than she is—'

'Age,' said Leah, 'has nothing to do with it.'

'I do think,' John ventured, 'that it is sometimes possible to see evil where no evil exists. If Edith had met more young men – if we had entertained more–'

'This is our home,' Leah said. 'Surely you don't want the world and his wife tramping through it!'

'I think Beth should be allowed to enjoy herself a little, that's all,' John said.

'Very well.' Leah nodded, her lips drawn down. 'If you are content to allow your sister to rampage around the countryside with some unknown bank clerk from nowhere, then I have no power to prevent it, but it's your responsibility.'

'I think it would be best.' He glanced placatingly at his sister. 'Beth is a good girl, not restless like Edith. She will not abuse a little freedom.'

'Upon my word,' Leah said with an angry little laugh, 'you talk as if I kept you all in prison. You have always been at liberty to do as you pleased.'

'I was not suggesting–'

'No, of course not. For heaven's sake, let us not begin to quarrel. I must put Teddy down for his nap.'

'Let me carry him. He's getting too heavy for you.'

John reached out to take his son but Leah evaded him, holding the child more firmly as she rose.

'I am not an invalid,' she said lightly. 'Anyway he is more used to me. Gentlemen always look so silly, carrying babies.'

'And you are wonderful with him.'

'He is a Falcon,' Leah said simply. 'Even if matters do not always fall out as I planned, I know that nobody could ever accuse me of anything less than the deepest devotion to my family.'

In the brown-curtained sitting-room above the school room Cousin Wenna was writing to her mother. She wrote in Welsh, the language they generally spoke at home, and her lips curved in a smile. Mam complained sometimes that everybody in the world got regular mail except them. She would be pleased to have all the news delivered in a large packet of closely written sheets.

–a good journey. You would enjoy riding on a train. Cousin John and sister met me at the station. He is a very elegant, quiet, young gentleman, shy in his manner. Cousin Beth is a strange girl. She seems very cheerful and content, but underneath there is something odd, as if she were likely to step through an invisible curtain and disappear. She was very friendly and told me that John's wife has just run away with Cousin Leah's husband. Can you imagine! Cousin Leah herself is dark and slim, very controlled in her manner. I met her this morning, though it's my belief she was not indisposed yesterday as she claimed but wished for a report on me before being introduced. She was very gracious, and asked after you kindly, but it's obvious that I am to consider myself a poor relation. However I fully intend to earn my salary. I saw John's child too. They have named him Edward (after the Prince of Wales, I suppose). He's a lively baby and Cousin Leah obviously dotes on him. I cannot understand how any woman could run off and abandon her child, but it takes all sorts!

Kingsmead, which is the main house, is very old and grand. Saron Farm would fit into a little corner of the great hall. Everything in the front part of the house has been left as it always was, with tapestries and stone floors, but there are two wings built on and these are lighter and more comfortably furnished.

Apart from Kingsmead itself the Falcons own a farm at the other side of the river. Cousin Edith, whom I've not yet met, lives there. It seems that she moved quite recently, having quarrelled with Leah. I mean to go over and make her acquaintance soon.

The school is a very handsome building, though I could wish it furnished more cheerfully, but the classroom on the first floor is big and airy, with space for about twenty pupils. My private apartments are above the classroom. I have a sitting-room with a kitchen leading out of it and there are two bedrooms, so if you could find somebody to take over the farm for a few weeks, it would be possible for you to come and stay.

The land around is pretty and heavily wooded in parts, but it lacks the grandeur of our hills. However I intend to take some long walks about the district, and Cousin John has given me the use of two horses.

My salary is to be two hundred pounds a year. I will be able to send some home to you every few months, so be sure to get a girl in to help with the heavy work. Maggie would be glad to earn a few coppers every week, and she's a fine, strong girl.

I forgot to tell you that Cousin Beth owns the cottage down by the river. Do you remember telling us how, when you were little, your mother mentioned a cottage she'd known called 'Witch's Dower'? That is the name of the cottage here, and the story they told me in the village today was that the Falcons have witch blood that came out of Wales! Did you ever hear the tale before?

I find folk very friendly here, not in the least stiff and starched as we feared English people would be. The village itself is very neatly tended – no chapels, but a church with an enormous graveyard. I intend to have a saunter round when the opportunity arises.

Her hand was aching a little. She laid down her pen and went over to the window. A long September twilight was stealing across the meadows. From where she stood she could see the drive winding between low bushes to the white gateposts beyond which the road reached towards the bridge that spanned the river.

She let the curtain drop back and returned to the desk. At this hour she and Mam would have milked the two cows, fed Toss the sheepdog, and would be sitting by the fire, mugs of tea in their hands and their skirts held up over their knees. Not long before there had been three of them.

Wenna sighed and shook her dead

husband out of her thoughts. No sense in mourning for Tom now. Grief never brought back the dead, and she had come to Marie Regina to start a new life.

She began to write again.

'I think I am going to be happy here, Mam, and I'm grateful that you didn't try to persuade me to stay at home with you. As you say it's a foolish thing to try to own the people we love, and I shall often write to you and let you know how everything is progressing.'

She would, she thought, have a great deal to do, for she had no idea how clever her pupils would be, and rather suspected that in some subjects she would be forced to work very hard in order to keep just a few pages ahead.

And she was anxious to get to know her English cousins. Beth and John had already shown themselves eager to be friendly, in contrast to Leah who had acted, Wenna thought with faint amusement, as if she, and not her brother, were owner of Kingsmead.

'I must go and lock up now. This house is big enough to take a walk through on a wet day! I am going into Maidstone to buy some ornaments for my sitting-room, to cheer the place a little...'

CHAPTER FOURTEEN

They had picnicked among the grey ruins, and ridden to Maidstone to buy new materials for the paintings, and walked through the cemetery to the great tomb, shaped like a house, without windows but with a triple locked door through which generations of dead Falcons had been carried. At the door a stone angel stood with uplifted wings and outstretched sword.

'I never liked that angel,' Beth said. 'It has a very spiteful expression, I think.'

'A slightly disgusted one,' Michael Shaw corrected.

'I'm not surprised,' Beth said. 'Some of my ancestors were really rather dreadful.'

'The tomb must be pretty crowded,' Michael said, reading the long list of engraved names.

'The last ones to be buried in it were my father's first wife and his stepmother,' Beth said. 'They were killed in an accident. Willow, that was the stepmother, was a cousin and had Falcon blood, and as she lay dying she said, "Victory will not come until a Falcon rides upon a moth". Wasn't that a strange thing to say?'

'Very strange,' he agreed.

'My own parents are buried here.' She indicated a nearby grave on which he read.

Sacred to the Memory
of
Lord Harry Falcon
Born 1836. Died 1884.
and of his wife,
Margred
Born 1842. Died 1885.

'My father was killed when his horse threw him,' Beth said softly, 'and Mam only lived a year afterwards. She wanted to be with him. That is love, isn't it?'

'Selfishness too,' Michael said, 'for she had a family.'

'There are always people to look after children,' Beth said. 'My brother's wife left him recently, and Leah is taking care of little Teddy. Sometimes I think it would have been easier for me if Mam had died when I was a baby, before I had learned to love her.'

'You miss her, don't you?' he said gently.

'She was very gay,' Beth said wistfully. 'She

was tiny but her hair was black, not mousy like mine. It was so long she could sit on it, and her eyes were yellow. Yellow as a cat's, and slanting up at the corners. She was very beautiful was Mam.'

'You too,' Michael said, looking at her, 'are beautiful. Not all the time, for nobody can be beautiful all the time, but there are flashes of loveliness in you. The longer I look at you the more often they come.'

'I am looking forward to seeing my portrait,' Beth said, flushing deeply and speaking very rapidly.

'I needed more time, so that I could have caught every changing expression in a dozen portraits,' he said.

'But the cottage is finished,' she reminded him.

'And I have a dozen sketches of the landscape from which I can make pastel studies. That will fill up the winter evenings.'

'I hate winter,' Beth said abruptly, beginning to thread her way between the headstones to the low stone wall beyond which the meadows stretched. 'I shall hate it even more this year.'

'Won't you go to balls and parties?' he enquired.

'At Kingsmead! Leah doesn't like social

life and my brother – he misses his wife very much.'

'How will you spend your time?'

'I'll go to Maidstone to borrow books from the library,' she said, 'and I'll keep "Witch's Dower" clean and aired, and I'll write to you – may I write to you?'

She had begun to scramble over the wall and half-turned, the silky material of her green bodice stretched tightly across her breasts, her tail of hair heavy against the whiteness of her neck.

'It will be better if you don't,' he said, and the finality of his tone brought the blood coursing into her face.

'Oh. I see,' she said, and became very busy in getting herself and her long skirt over the close set stones.

'You don't see,' he contradicted, and caught at her hand. 'You don't see at all. If it meant nothing to me then I would be very happy to have you write to me. But when I leave here I won't be coming back and it would hurt too much to be reminded. Can you understand what I'm trying to say to you?'

'That this is a part out of your real life, a kind of dream that has to be forgotten,' she said.

'Not forgotten. I never will forget it,' he told her.

'But you won't come back,' she said, and began to walk very fast across the grass, her skirt rustling.

'You knew it would be so.' He lengthened his stride and spoke, almost pleadingly, to her averted profile. 'We met by chance and have enjoyed a very pleasant time together. I have truly appreciated your company.'

'But I don't believe that,' she said, without looking at him. 'I don't believe we met by chance. Ever since I was a little girl I've wished upon the moon for things I've wanted very badly. And the moon has listened for I was born as she was rising, and I have the devil's kiss on my thigh. And I wished for a man to ride into my life and show me what it is like to be loved. And you came, you see.'

'And I will ride away,' he said.

'Then we had best finish the portrait,' she said. 'You told me that it needs only a few touches.'

They had reached the main road and she broke into a run, hurrying across to the bridle path and vanishing among the trees as her green dress blended with the leaves.

He followed slowly, his head bent, and

going into the cottage found her in the herb-room. There were tearstains on her round cheeks but she held her head high.

'I never told your fortune,' she said. 'My mother left me a crystal that once belonged to a gypsy. I see events in it, not clearly, and never for myself, I can never see for myself.'

'You live too much in dreams,' he told her.

'That should suit you,' she retorted, 'for in your view I'm only a dream myself. You will be glad to wake up, I daresay, when you return to London. You will say to your wife, "Oh, I met a most amusing young creature, my dear. She ran around after me like a puppy wagging its tail" and she will smile and pour you another cup of tea.'

'You know that isn't so,' he interrupted.

'Then tell me how it will be. Tell me.'

'I will hold your image in my mind,' he said slowly. 'I will think of this dream as the most real part of my life, and value the memory.'

'You're content with very little,' Beth said scornfully. 'And you would leave me with very little too.'

'You have the rest of your life.'

'And much longer than you in which to be lonely.'

'You'll marry.'

'Not where I cannot love. I'll not do that.'

'Many women do, and many of the marriages turn out happily.'

'That's city talk,' Beth said scornfully.

'I'm a city man,' Michael said, smiling. 'Don't you think I look like a nice, respectable, city man?'

'I don't know what you look like,' she said slowly. 'When I first met you by day, I could have described you very clearly, but since that first time I have never looked at you in the same way. It's as if my feelings for you coloured my sight.'

'For me too,' he said, and they looked at each other across the space that divided them.

'I'll tell your fortune,' Beth said, afraid of the silence. 'I haven't shown you my crystal yet.'

She darted to the cupboard and brought down the leather bag. He went over and watched her pull out the crystal, holding it carefully between her hands.

'So that was your mother's too?' He touched the back of her hand with his fingers.

'An old gypsy gave it to her. Mam could see things in it sometimes, and so can I.'

She went over to the window seat and held

265

the crystal on her lap. The sunshine, forcing its way through creeper, cast green light on her hair and hands. For a reason he couldn't understand, Michael shivered. The idea had entered his head that, in a moment, the girl with the crystal would raise her head, and it would not be Beth at all but somebody quite different.

'There is nothing to see,' Beth said, in a perfectly normal, vexed tone. 'There is absolutely nothing there.'

'Perhaps I have no future,' he said lightly.

'Or it is linked with mine. I could never see anything for myself.'

Beth rose and, coming back to the table, put the crystal into the bag and replaced it on the shelf.

'Shall I make you some tea?' she asked.

'If you like. Won't your family be expecting you?'

'They're away,' she said. 'John went up to London this morning and Leah went with him. She has to buy things for the baby, and she likes the London shops even though she's not fond of the city itself. I am free and independent until tomorrow evening. If I don't go home the servants will assume I stayed with Edith at Whittle Farm.'

'Your name,' he said wryly, following her

into the sitting-room, 'ought to be Eve.'

'Why Eve?' Measuring out tea, she slanted a look at him.

'Who was it who tempted Adam?'

'And who tempted Eve in the first place? Would you,' she enquired demurely, 'like some stewed apples for your tea?'

He laughed, his dark face lighting into youthfulness again.

'You ought to laugh more often,' Beth approved.

'I am out of the habit,' he told her. 'There is not much laughter in our house.'

'But this is mine.' Setting cups on the table, she said, breathlessly as if she had been running. 'There will always be laughter here – and a place for you.'

'I am going back to London early tomorrow morning,' he said, the laughter dying in his face. 'I am going back to Susan. There is no other way.'

'But we have tonight,' Beth said, and gave him a bright, wide smile that had in it something infinitely gallant.

They sat down to eat, each carefully avoiding the other's eyes, not touching as they passed cups and plates.

'You still have five days,' Beth said. 'You could stay on for five days.'

267

'Best that I go home,' he said briefly. 'You will apologize to your sister and brother for me, won't you?'

'Yes. Yes, of course.'

'And in a year or two I will read an account in the newspaper of a smart Society wedding.'

'No,' she said flatly, and the cup rattled slightly as she put it back into the saucer.

'My dear, it's best for me to leave,' Michael said. 'It's best that I don't write to you nor you to me. It's best.'

'Yes, of course,' she said brightly.

'And you will forget me,' he said.

'I wish,' Beth said lightly, 'that you would stop telling me what I will or won't do. You are only trying to convince yourself, you know.'

'I know,' he said sombrely, and she paused in the act of lighting the lamp, and gazed at him. There was no reason for hope, but it rose up in her all the same.

The light had faded rapidly and a wind ruffled the wood. The sky was a mixture of grey and silver and the bridle path narrowed into blackness. Against the tiny panes of the window the girl's figure was outlined but her face was in shadow.

'If anything very bad ever happened, if

ever I needed you,' she said.

'Nothing will happen,' he interrupted.

'No, of course not, but if it did, would you come back? I'd not embarrass you by writing. I'd not intrude on your life, but if the need was very great would you come?'

'How would I know?' he asked. 'I have no crystal.'

'I'll send the moonstone ring,' she said. 'If that ever comes, then you'll know that I need you too much to be able to bear it any longer.'

'By God, I want you,' Michael said, not loudly but in a tone of such suppressed passion that she stared at him, her eyes big in the fading light.

'You can wish on the moon,' she said at last, and her voice trembled between laughter and tears.

'Wish for me. Wish for us both,' he urged.

Beyond the window the moon was rising above the trees. Beth turned to look at it and Michael came to stand behind her. She could feel his breath on her neck, and her own breathing quickened. The palms of her hands were damp but her mouth was dry as if she thirsted. Through her mind, as if she were drowning, flashed her happy childhood when Mam had sang her songs of mountains and maidens in the lilting language of her own girlhood.

'You and I,' Mam had said, 'bear the mark. People laugh at such things these days, but the wise keep silent. Remember you can waste your gift or use it well; you can love many times or choose one love for your whole life through as I did.'

That had been one of the last occasions on which she and Mam had talked together. After that Mam had begun to brush her hair again and to sit for long hours with a listening look on her face. And soon afterwards she had died and the song had ceased, or perhaps been sung again in another place.

'Wish for us both,' Michael said.

'Moon, I wish to love and be loved,' Beth said aloud. Michael had stepped away from her, and in his voice was her final chance of refusal.

'Nothing can change. I will still return to London,' he said. 'The way we feel cannot alter the lives we lead. I have nothing to offer.'

It seemed to Beth in that moment that for the first time the cottage was full of others, shadows who moved in and out as if they wove some strange and secret dance. Long-haired girls in unfamiliar dresses chose love, and filled the old house with weeping and laughter with none to tell which would last the longer.

'I choose this night,' Beth said, and her hands moved to the fastenings on her dress as she turned to face him again.

The conventions in which she had been reared, the thought of Leah's disgust at such abandoned behaviour, her own shyness, were whirled away as the blood of her ancestors coursed through her veins, and her garments were shed at her feet as if they were skins from which her true self emerged.

The air struck chill on her bare flesh, but she moved without haste savouring these moments that bridged girlhood from womanhood. As she walked towards the stairs and began to climb them she looked back once in silent invitation.

Michael went over and began to pick up the scattered clothes. Each garment was warm, imbued with her faint, female smell. After long years of continence his own nature was awake and craving.

He took a final glance at the horned moon and then followed her up the narrow stairs.

Evening brooded into night, the sky

purpling into blackness, the flowers becoming pale ghosts against the darker shapes of bush and tree. A fox, brush uplifted, mask pointed upriver, slunk along the bank and paused for an instant as if some instinct of its animal nature had felt for one heartbeat of time an alien mating call.

The wind swept around the eaves of 'Witch's Dower' and was gone, leaving the creepers to settle more closely about the walls. In the long grass beyond the clearing fireflies swooped and darted in spirals of ecstasy.

In the herb-room shadows without faces crowded together out of the memory-soaked walls, and a murmuring of ancient timber mingled with the whispering of voices from other centuries, and there was the scent of honey like a promise on the air.

The night paced out its span, the moon triumphant amid attendant stars, the darkness enfolding the little, creeping things. Towards dawn a light rain began to fall, stirring the creepers, drumming on the roof, hazing the banks of the river.

The light grew stronger, obscuring the pale crowned moon, sending gleams of early sunshine arrowing the rain so that the haze over the river was riddled with gold.

'If we could hold back time,' Beth said, 'would you not do so?'

'Sweetheart, it's not possible,' Michael told her.

He was already dressing, and she lay in the warm space from which he had just risen and watched him. It seemed to her that part of him had already left and was speeding ahead along the London road towards a life in which she was of no importance. His face was beginning to settle into the lines of frustrated resignation that characterized his usual expression.

'You will come if ever I send the moonstone?' she asked in fear.

'You have my word.'

'I'll not send unless the matter be so urgent that I have great need.'

'I know that. You didn't have to say it.'

At that moment she would have said anything to keep him by her side for a few minutes longer.

'The pictures are downstairs. The one of you is not quite finished, but if I were to paint you now you would look different,' Michael said.

'How different?'

'As different as a ripe apple is from a green

one,' he said.

There was the shadow of a smile in his voice, but the haunted look was still in his eyes.

'You must not regret what has happened between us,' she said quickly. 'I would not have you remember me with regret.'

'I will remember you with love,' he said, and reached over to touch her cheek with his hand.

She closed her eyes briefly, fighting back the impulse to beg him to stay. Had she been in his place she would have shrugged off her old life like a shabby coat and taken happiness with both hands, but men were settled creatures who clung to their security even when it was empty of love.

When she opened her eyes Michael was standing by the door.

'God bless you, my love,' he said, but it was a stranger with a disillusioned face who spoke the words, as if her lover had already left.

Beth nodded, smiling, thinking that if he did not touch her once more she would wither into loneliness all the sooner, thinking that if he did touch her she would break into uncountable pieces.

He turned and went out of the door, and she crouched upon the bed, her eyes fixed upon the empty space, her ears catching each separate footstep as it descended. The front door closed and from outside came the jangling of harness and the retreating of hoofbeats over soft, rain-soaked earth.

When there was no more sound beyond the pattering of the sun-streaked rain, Beth wrapped a blanket about herself and went downstairs into the living-room. The dead ashes of the fire and the unwashed dishes were all that remained of the warmth and the meal they had shared.

Her clothes lay over the back of a chair. Beth felt them but they were cold and limp, retaining nothing of the hands that had put them there. She dressed slowly, her fingers stiff and clumsy.

'If I think of him very hard with very great love,' she told herself, 'he will come back to me and tell me that he loves me too much to leave.'

She had finished dressing but the cottage was still silent.

'If I send out my longing he will come back. If I wish once more on the moon—'

She flung wide the door, but rain blurred the clearing and the moon had fled. She would have to wait until nightfall before she could wish again, and by then Michael would be at home. He would walk into a house she had never seen and greet a woman she would never meet. 'One night,' Beth said aloud, 'is not sufficient. There will be other nights or I will not be able to bear it.'

The pictures he had painted were propped against the wall. The one of the cottage she had already seen but she looked at it again, remembering how surely his fingers had guided the brush across the canvas. The small house gleamed like a pearl in the sunlit green clearing.

The other portrait was the one of herself which she had not seen. She took up the canvas and sat down at the table to study it.

The background was not finished and her face gazed back at her through pale swirling clouds. A young, round face with eyes half-closed as if she felt the warmth of the sun, a tail of honey-coloured hair curling down the side of her neck, and one hand lightly brushed in with a moonstone gleaming against the flesh.

It was not signed, but anyone who looked would know, if they had eyes to see, that the artist had painted his subject with love.

Beth took the small canvas into the herb-room and placed it high on the shelf next to the drawstring bag in which she kept the crystal and the little jar of mandrake powder.

She would keep it there until Michael came back. Suddenly, without reason, she knew that he would come back. He had left the portrait unfinished as a pledge. The rain was stopping, and the sun, gaining strength, flooded the herb-room, gilding her hands as she held them out into the shaft of dust-dancing brilliance.

'Oh, Michael, if you were here,' she said pleadingly, 'you would want to paint this.'

But Michael was on his way back to a woman he didn't love and she didn't know. The sunshine would be drying the rain on his heavy travelling cloak, and the brim of his hat would shield the dark, clearcut features that she had known for such a short space.

She began to cry, the sobs racking her body, her hands held out in the sunlight as if she were blind. She was so full of pain and loneliness that crying brought no relief at all, and in her mind the face of her lover grew dimmer as if his image receded in time with the galloping of hoofs along the London road. The sun rose higher, until every corner of the room was a mocking golden.

CHAPTER FIFTEEN

'That was an excellent supper. You are a splendid cook, Cousin Wenna.'

John leaned back and smiled at Wenna, who refilled his coffee cup, and nodded her head in acknowledgement of the compliment.

'I enjoy cooking,' she said in her forthright, pleasant manner. 'I like eating too. There are so many blessings in life, if that doesn't sound pious.'

'It sounds,' he said smiling, 'as if you have a happy disposition.'

'Ah! but I've been fortunate,' she said. 'My childhood was a very happy one, and my marriage was happy though it didn't last very long with Tom being killed so young. I'm sorry! I ought to have remembered.'

'That my marriage was not happy? I believed that it was, you know. I truly believed Grace was content with me.'

'What was she like?' Wenna asked.

'Very beautiful,' he said. 'A tall young lady, with eyes that were dark blue, and red hair.

Naturally red, and not tinted as some actresses have it. She was an actress, you know. A dancer. I never saw her on the stage. If she had continued I am sure she would have been successful, for she was so full of spirit and energy.'

'You talk as if she were dead,' Wenna said.

'I suppose because to me she is,' John said slowly. 'She was a friend of Leah's, you know. They met when Leah was in town on a shopping expedition. We were married quite soon afterwards.'

'I can't imagine Leah having a woman friend,' Wenna said frankly.

'Oh, my sister has had to carry more than her share of responsibility,' John said quickly. 'She has had little time or inclination for social life. I suppose you find it hard to imagine me the husband of an actress.'

Wenna studied him thoughtfully, her green eyes critical. He was, she thought, a good-looking man though there was a weakness about his mouth. And his nature was gentle, yet there was a suspicion of recklessness in him to judge from the tale he had told. It had surely been reckless to marry an actress on what seemed to have been a very short acquaintance.

'Will you divorce her?' she asked.

'At first, after she had gone, I said I would not. I hoped she would come back, you see, and I would have forgiven her and we could have gone on, not as before but a little wiser.'

'And now?'

'Now I feel she will never come back. It would be foolish for a man to wait all his life for a woman who didn't love him. And she may wish to be legally free. It would be pure selfishness on my part to bind her when she might wish to re-marry.'

'You might wish to re-marry yourself one day,' Wenna suggested.

'I am not the world's greatest success with ladies,' John said wryly. 'My brother, Price, can charm every female he meets, but I was always tied up with the management of the estate and my duties in the House. You know, these evenings when we sit here, comfortably talking over the events of the day, mean a great deal to me. You have fitted in so well here.'

'I like teaching,' Wenna said simply. 'The children can be so funny and so sweet. And I like Marie Regina, even if the villagers do regard me as a foreigner.'

'Kentish folk take their time,' John said. 'I hope you have not found us stiff and snobbish. My sister would have invited you up to the house much oftener, but she has not been well and with her child due in two months–' He spread his hands.

'Your other sister, Edith, is due in two months also, isn't she?'

'Poor Edith! She insisted upon remaining here. I tried to induce her to leave, for a while at least, but she would not.'

'There have been bastard children and unknown fathers before,' Wenna said sensibly.

'But the father is – I ought not to tell you this, but as you're a member of the family...' John hesitated, then plunged on. 'My sister's husband betrayed Edith before he eloped with Grace.'

'He sounds even more fatal to my sex than your brother Price,' Wenna said dryly.

'It is no joking matter,' John began, but an unwilling smile tugged at the corners of his mouth.

'When things are very bad, the only sensible course is to laugh at them,' Wenna said. 'But then I'm not concerned directly with these matters. I'm the poor widow who sits in the corner giving advice to everybody else.'

'Until you marry again. You are the sort of

woman who was born to be a wife.'

'How can you possibly tell the sort of woman I am?' she demanded in amusement. 'You know nothing of me.'

'I know that you are fond of children and can earn their respect and liking,' he said warmly. 'I know you are good tempered and truthful and when I am with you I feel – comfortable. Even this room seems different since you came.'

He glanced round the sitting-room. Cushions in green and blue now piled the couch, a vase of painted ferns occupied a small table near the brown curtains, there were books of various sizes in untidy piles along the top of the bookcase, and an embroidered quilt was hung like a tapestry against one wall.

'I bought a few things to make the place more my own,' Wenna said. 'It pleases me if you like them too.'

'I like them because they reflect your tastes,' he said shyly.

'You're very kind,' Wenna said, and her square, capable hand covered his own for a moment. 'It is a rare quality in a man. Beth tells me you have made over Whittle Farm as a gift to Edith.'

'I wished her to have security of tenure,'

he explained. 'Leah was not happy about it for it diminishes Teddy's inheritance, but the farm was acquired after the original entail and is mine to dispose of as I please.'

'Teddy is a fine child.'

'He's my pride and joy,' John said. 'If nothing had resulted from my marriage but Teddy, it would still have been worthwhile. The one thing I cannot forgive Grace is that she abandoned him.'

'But Leah dotes on him?'

'Obsessively,' John looked faintly surprised at his own choice of word, but went on, as if he were thinking aloud. 'She will scarcely allow him out of her sight. There are times when I believe she thinks more of Teddy than of her own coming child. Sometimes I feel it is – not altogether healthy.'

'You should divorce your wife and marry again,' Wenna said in her forthright manner.

'It would take time, perhaps several years. If there was a woman, do you think she would wait?'

'I think she would be happy to wait, until she was certain of her own feelings,' Wenna said.

This time his hand reached out to hers and lingered for a moment.

'And Beth? How is Beth?' Wenna moved

to poke the fire into a blaze.

'She is not well either,' John frowned. 'You know, Beth has always been an odd, dreamy sort of girl. She was very close to Mam, and Mam filled her head with old tales about the family. She needs more company but with matters as they are there is nobody to chaperone her into Society. Recently she has been very quiet and still, and once or twice I've come across her in tears.'

'Growing pains. Girls often suffer from them.'

'You know, I did hope that the gentleman to whom she rented the cottage – but it appears that he was married.'

'I had not thought of you in the role of matchmaker,' Wenna said amused.

'I would like Beth to be happy,' he said with a touch of wistfulness. 'I feel we made mistakes with Edith, but Leah was always fearful that Edith was too flighty to settle. Beth – I would like Beth to be wed. And there is a precedent for such a wedding for one of my own ancestors once allowed a gentleman to occupy "Witch's Dower", and eventually they were married.'

'And became my great-grandparents,' Wenna finished. 'Apple Falcon and her husband are buried together on Saron

Farm, he was called Geraint.'

'The Falcons have been in the habit of marrying their cousins,' John said. 'Leah feels strongly that this is not a good thing.'

'Leah feels strongly about a great many things,' Wenna said.

'Yes.' John hesitated as if he were about to say something more but evidently changed his mind and rose, saying instead, 'I must go now. The roads are bad this winter. Have you everything you need?'

'I have so many supplies that I could withstand a siege,' Wenna told him.

He lingered a few minutes longer, talking of this and that, reluctant to ride out. When he had gone she went over to the window to wave to him as he trotted down the snow-covered drive. As she let the curtain fall back into place her green eyes grew thoughtful. A man like John Falcon needed a wife; not a flighty red-haired actress but a sensible, kind-hearted woman who would encourage him to think for himself and build up his self-respect. For a moment impatience touched her and then was gone. She was young and could afford to wait.

Leah, her seven months pregnancy concealed under a flowing shawl, was in the solar, checking the letters that Annie or one of the grooms would take down into the village the following morning.

There were two letters from John to his peers in the House which she put back into the salver for onward delivery.

There was another letter from Beth to Michael Shaw, care of Nicholson's Bank, London. Leah's mouth tightened as she slit it open. This was the second letter that she had been forced to confiscate. The contents of the first one had shocked her inexpressibly. That Beth should have allowed herself to be seduced by a married man old enough to be her father! And now, without dignity or pride, she was begging him to help her because she was with child. In the midst of her disgust Leah felt a curious sense of satisfaction at having been proved right.

'Dear Michael,

Forgive me for writing to you again. I know I said I would never write to you at all, nor intrude on your real life. I am not asking you to come back to me. I know your duty lies elsewhere. But if you could send me one word to tell me that you still thought of me sometimes, then I would be proud to bear your child, knowing it a child of love and not the result of an episode you wanted to forget. One friendly note would set my mind at ease, for I will have to tell my family soon. Indeed I think Leah half-suspects already–'

There was more of it in Beth's round, childish writing. Leah read carefully to the end, noted two spelling mistakes, and locked it away at the back of the dresser in a narrow drawer that had once held small coins to be used for the day-to-day running of the household in Tudor times.

Beth would not be able to marry the man for he already had a wife. The prospect of her living with him in open adultery could not, of course, be entertained. If there was to be a scandal, then let it be confined within the family. Let it not spread beyond the village. What Beth had done proved she was unfit to be married, but that did not alter the fact that Leah had a duty to her and to the unborn child. Another Falcon, but with fresh blood to strengthen the stock. It was a thrilling prospect. Leah, her ears pricked for Teddy's cry, thought, with a certain amount of modest pride,

'I am a born mother. Even if my marriage failed, there will always be children around for me to guide and rear.'

She sighed and leaned back in her chair,

287

her eyes closing briefly. The last months had wearied her, for Teddy was a demanding child and had been cutting his teeth. She had taken on the night nursing herself, pacing the floor hour after hour with the baby held against her shoulder. Of Paul she refused to think. His desertion had swept away her last traces of romantic feeling. The man she had chosen hoping to develop and nurture his talents, had grossly deceived her. If he entered her mind at all she thrust him out again and turned her attention to the child.

She had neither seen nor spoken with Edith since her sister had moved to Whittle Farm. The vicar had come to Kingsmead, metaphorically wringing his hands, to be faced by an uncompromising refusal from Leah to discuss private family affairs.

'My unfortunate sister has chosen to reside at Whittle Farm. Her behaviour has been very unfortunate, but we have great troubles at present in the family and I do not propose to discuss those either.'

John had visited Edith frequently and had even taken the step of handing the farm over to her as a gift. He had brushed aside Leah's objections that he was depriving Teddy of part of his inheritance with the comment that a thousand acres ought to be enough for a babe.

John, Leah thought, was becoming much more independent. She had noticed a new authority in his bearing recently, a swing in his stride that hinted that he was not completely crushed by Grace's leaving. He was also spending a great deal of time at the school.

From considering John Leah fell to considering Wenna. Her cousin was, she thought, a pleasant, sensible young woman who had made an excellent start as schoolmistress. The women in the village regarded her, if not with open friendliness, at least without suspicion. She had, so far, conducted herself like a lady. But she was young, only about twenty or twenty-two and John was not yet twenty-five.

John's step was heard in the hall and she straightened her shoulders and called out:

'I'm in here, John! In the solar.'

'You haven't been waiting up for me?' He came in, rubbing his hands, smelling of cold and snow, and bent to kiss her cheek.

'I thought you might require a hot drink.'

'Wenna filled me with coffee, to top an excellent supper. Has Teddy been good?'

'Very good. You don't need anything then?'

'Annie can bring it if I do. You worry too much,' John said, peeling off his cape and sending flakes of melting snow over the carpet.

Leah curbed an annoyed comment and went out into the hall. Beth had come into her thoughts again, and she went upstairs with the intention of finding her sister. Very soon Beth's condition would become obvious, and she might be tempted to do something impulsive and silly.

Beth was in the large bedroom she had shared with Edith until the latter had left Kingsmead. The lamp had been lit and a fire glowed in the hearth, but the atmosphere was cheerless.

The girl looked plain, Leah thought. Her eyelids were swollen, and her hair was lank, tied back carelessly with a black ribbon.

'You didn't eat very much at supper,' Leah said, taking the chair opposite her sister. 'Are you not well?'

'I wasn't hungry,' Beth said shortly.

'My dear, can't you tell me what is troubling you?' Leah asked gently. 'It's been clear for a long time that something is very wrong. I wish you could bring yourself to confide in me.'

'I cannot, I cannot,' Beth said, and began

to cry again, softly and steadily.

'Is it to do with the gentleman who stayed at the cottage?' Leah asked. 'I fancied that you seemed – taken with him? Perhaps I am wrong but–'

'I am carrying his child,' Beth said.

She had stopped crying and her voice was husky.

'I see,' Leah leaned forward and laid her hand over Beth's cold, damp ones. 'I was afraid of something like this happening, and I blame myself for having allowed you to go about unchaperoned, but his betrayal of you is very shocking.'

'It was no betrayal,' Beth said. 'We fell in love. I know he loved me, and I shall always love him. He would have married me, Leah, if he had been free. I know he would.'

'His duty lay with his wife. He surely recognized that.'

'We both recognized it,' Beth said. 'I let him go to her, didn't I?'

'Because you couldn't prevent it?'

'I suppose so,' Beth said reluctantly. 'But he'll come back to me, if I truly need him. I know he will.'

'Does he know about the child?'

'I wrote to him,' Beth said miserably. 'I've written twice, not to his home for I don't know that address, but to the bank where he works. I didn't ask him to leave his wife or come back to me, but it's his baby and he has a right to know.'

'It is a Falcon child,' Leah said, 'like Teddy and the child I carry, and Edith's baby too. A new generation of Falcon children growing up in our ancient home. Children all round us, Beth.'

'And three of them without fathers,' Beth sobbed.

'It is mothers who are important,' Leah said. 'It is women who have the strongest natures, my dear. I was – deserted as you and Edith have been.'

'I was not deserted,' Beth said with a flash of spirit. 'We agreed to part.'

'And I take it he has not answered your letters?'

'Perhaps they didn't reach him. Letters often go astray,' Beth said hopefully.

'You don't really believe that, do you?' Leah asked.

'He loves me. He still loves me,' Beth said.

'Perhaps so, but think for a moment,' Leah urged. 'A man may fall in love and be flattered by the attentions of a pretty young woman, but he is not going to be very pleased when a letter from her arrives, informing him that he is going to be a father. Men can set love aside and go on with their lives. We women must learn the same strength.'

'I was hoping–' Beth's head drooped and her tears began to fall again.

'And kept everything to yourself without allowing me to help you.'

Leah's tone was gently reproachful.

'There has been so much scandal in the family,' Beth said tremblingly.

'Then a little more will scarcely matter,' Leah soothed. 'The child is due in – June, I suppose?'

Beth nodded, rubbing her eyes childishly with the backs of her hands. When she looked up there was a tremulous smile on her mouth.

'You've been very good to me, Leah,' she said softly. 'I'm sorry for having brought disgrace upon the family, but I *was* loved, and I can't be sorry about that. And he still loves me. I have to go on believing that.'

'No doubt he does,' said Leah.

'I wished on the moon,' Beth said. 'I wished to love and be loved, and my wish was granted, Leah. It was.'

'You'd best go to bed,' Leah said, patting the younger girl's shoulder. 'It does you and the child no good to sit fretting. Why, we could all sit down and weep if we lost our courage. And if you love this – what was his name?'

'Shaw. Michael Shaw.'

'If you love him, you'll not wish to cause him trouble by writing to his bank,' Leah said. 'You'll find the strength to bear his child alone, as I will bear mine.'

'And Edith hers.'

'Edith too,' Leah said coldly, 'though I cannot forgive her deception of me.'

'You've been very good,' Beth said again. 'I don't know how John will take it. He's had so much trouble.'

'Leave John to me,' Leah said briskly. 'Go to sleep now and try not to worry too much, dear.'

Folding her shawl about her, Leah went slowly to the door, her skirts rustling purposefully over the carpet, her head tilted back slightly from the weight of her chignon.

Beth rose also and went over to the window, leaning her head wearily against the cold panes. Beyond the glass the world stretched white to the fringe of trees that marked the beginning of the deerpark. The moon was full tonight, its face wise and evil.

Beth shook her head slightly, wondering why the word 'evil' had come into her mind.

'Moon, make him come back to Kings-mead,' she whispered. 'Make him come back.'

She could see Michael's face so clearly that it was as if he stood just behind a sheet of glass. A loving expression imparted youthfulness to his eyes and mouth, and he looked as if he were about to speak to her. Hope rose up in her and with it such an agony of longing that she put her fingers in her mouth and bit down upon them until tears of pain came into her eyes.

The apartment was too big for one person. She missed Edith's company, for the other had been gay and pleasant when she was not in a sulking humour. But Edith slept alone now at Whittle Farm, and Leah paced the floor with Teddy in her arms, and Michael – where was Michael?

Comfortably asleep with his unloved Susan at his side? Or did he toss and turn, thinking of the letter that he would have already received, and in turning reach out and accidentally touch his wife?

Beth took one last, pleading look at the moon. Its expression now was benign. She wondered how she could have imagined it evil.

The fire was burning lower and the lamp

flickered as if an unseen hand had waved across it. She saw that snow was beginning to fall again, obscuring sky and moon and trees. The landscape was blotted out in whirling whiteness.

'He'll come back,' Beth said aloud to the empty room. 'He will come back. When spring comes, when the bluebells come out in the woods by "Witch's Dower", he'll come back to me then. He'll choose love before duty. I know it.'

She began to undress, slowly and tiredly, relief at having found Leah so kind mingling with the pain of separation. The words she had just spoken wove themselves into a pattern of hope in her mind.

CHAPTER SIXTEEN

'Nothing has been said to me about the affair,' Wenna told John. 'The villagers may gossip among themselves, but to a stranger they will say nothing. Anyway, I am a member of the family, in a remote way, and so they would assume that I knew all the details.'

'Not so remote. You are Mam's cousin, and a second cousin to me.'

'A friend too, I hope?'

'A very close and dear friend,' he said warmly. 'You cannot know what your friendship means to me.'

'This has been a bad year for you,' Wenna said with sympathy. 'A wife gone, a sister deserted, two sisters betrayed.'

'Poor little Beth! I ought to have known the man was not to be trusted.' John's eyes were unhappy. 'I was for going to see him, but Leah convinced me that it would do no good. We must protect Beth and her coming child.'

'But the other babes are well?' she queried. 'Edith's and Leah's?'

'Caleb and Mary, born on the same day, of the same father. I find that ironic.'

'Was Leah disappointed that her babe was a girl?'

'She was pleased, I think. Teddy is like her own child. Edith declares that her boy is to be known as Cal Falcon. She continues very defiant.'

John sighed as he spoke, for at his last visit to the farm, Edith had said:

'Leah married the man I wanted. Now, as Cal grows up, she will always be reminded that he loved me at least as much as he ever loved her.'

'And Beth is well?'

'Silent and often tearful. There are two months more of waiting for her.'

'So much trouble, but it can't last.' Wenna tried to draw him into her own cheerfulness. 'Spring is here, and the babes are healthy, and this will all dwindle into a nine days wonder very soon.'

'I have begun divorce proceedings against Grace,' John said abruptly.

'Oh?'

'It will be heard in the House of Lords, my being a peer. More scandal.'

'It will be painful for you.'

'Not as painful as I imagined it might be, once I made my mind up to it. She will have to be traced, she and Paul Simmons so that they may defend if they choose, but I think it unlikely. It may take two or three years before I am legally free, but when I am, is it possible that you might–?'

He hesitated, a flush spreading over his face, his eyes anxious.

'I am a very patient woman,' Wenna said.

'And we are already good friends.'

'The best of friends,' she assured him.

'You like children, don't you? Teddy is–'

'I love children, and I would be very disappointed in you if you did not regard your first-born as the most remarkable baby who ever breathed,' she told him. 'But I would like children of my own too one day.'

'As many as you please,' he assured her.

Always, he thought, did she succeed in drawing him into her own tranquil mood. There was a quaint strength in this Welsh cousin which brought out the latent strength in himself. It was hard to define in his own mind but when he was with her he felt himself to be more of a man, more in control of his own destiny.

He rode back to Kingsmead slowly, his own optimism reviving with the flowers of spring. After the harsh winter the thaw had come gently, swelling the river, urging on grass and blossom.

The great house dreamed in spring sunshine. He looked at it with affection as he dismounted in the courtyard, and for the first time, thought not of Grace coming out to the step to meet him but of Wenna with her kind smile and sleepy eyes.

Leah was, as usual in the solar. She had borne her daughter easily and, trimly corseted, was reading the day's mail. As her brother came in she looked up and said:

'Try not to stamp upstairs. Teddy had me up before dawn and Mary has only just gone off to sleep.'

'You should let Beth help.'

'Beth is lying down. She is not eating enough to put flesh on a lark! You've been over to see Edith, I suppose?'

'She's well,' he said briefly, aware of Leah's disapproval. 'Cal is a fine baby.'

'Caleb,' Leah sniffed, 'I cannot imagine what possessed her to choose such a rustic name. Did you call at the school?'

'I looked in. Cousin Wenna sent her regards.'

'She is well, I take it?'

'Very well. It is a treat to see a young woman so healthy and contented.'

He had gone over to the window and, looking out into the courtyard, said abruptly:

'I have decided to divorce Grace.'

'To break your marriage vows?' she said sharply.

'It was she who broke them,' John reminded her. 'I am not doing this out of a spirit of revenge, my dear sister. I know that divorce is a terrible thing and that it will be a further grief to you when the name of her lover is made public.'

'I was not asking you to consider me,'

300

Leah said. 'But I do think you should consider Teddy.'

'I cannot see how divorce can be blamed upon a child,' he argued. 'Teddy will be known as the son of a woman who abandoned him anyway. Is he to be deprived of a mother and I of a second wife through social convention?'

Behind him Leah sat very still, her hands locked together.

'Am I to understand that you are thinking of marrying again?' she asked lightly.

'Not immediately, of course. The divorce may take years. But we are still young and time can strengthen affection.'

'We?'

'Cousin Wenna and I–' he began.

'Of course,' Leah let out her breath in a small sigh. 'You have become very fond of Cousin Wenna.'

'She is a splendid person!' He turned to face Leah, his voice and bearing full of enthusiasm. 'It is so peaceful in her company. Grace – she never belonged here. She was never part of the Falcons.'

'She was more closely connected with the family than either of us guessed,' Leah said slowly.

'What on earth do you mean?'

'A letter came from Price this morning.'

'From South Africa? How is he?'

'In the rudest health, apparently the letter was for me but a paragraph in it concerns you.' She consulted the letter that lay before her on the desk. 'He writes – "What is all this about John marrying a Grace Finn? Now that I'm at a safe distance from your disapproval, my dear Leah, I can tell you that I was keeping a red-haired charmer called Grace Finn in a little apartment in Bayswater. We broke up amicably when my debts became too pressing, but how on earth did John come to marry her?" Price always uses such vulgar expressions,' Leah said.

'I don't understand.' John was staring at her in bewilderment. 'Grace and Price? You told me that you met her in the milliners.'

'We got into conversation there. If I remember rightly it was she who spoke first to me. I suppose she recognized me, or followed me, and wished to speak to me out of curiosity. She did not, of course, mention that she knew Price. And to think that I innocently invited her to Kingsmead as your prospective bride when she had just finished a clandestine affair with your own brother! John, we have been most cruelly deceived!'

'It makes no sense,' he said. 'Why should she agree to marry me?'

'To provide a father for her child,' Leah said, and put her hand up to her mouth.

'Her child?' John said blandly.

'Oh, my God! the words just came to me.' She rose in an agitated manner, her eyes anguished. 'John, don't you see? She must have been expecting Price's child when he went to South Africa. And I went and offered to introduce her to you. She must have been laughing up her sleeve at us all.'

'But if anyone had discovered–?'

'It was a justifiable risk for her,' Leah said. 'Price was in South Africa and unlikely to return for years. Mail takes a very long time. Why, when I told Price you were wed, I don't believe I even mentioned the lady's surname. But Edith has written to him, it seems, with a catalogue of woes, and he is naturally very puzzled.'

'But I wrote to Price myself.'

'The letter must have gone astray. He is moving about and letters take a long time to catch up with him.'

'Teddy is my son,' John said suddenly.

'My dear, we have both believed so,' Leah said sadly.

'He is my son,' John repeated.

'A seven months' child,' Leah said.

'My son.'

'John, we must face facts! You know the conversation we had in this very room, when you told me what the specialist had said?'

'You told me that he was wrong.'

'I thought he must be. I could not believe – I was so sure that the right sort of wife would enable you to – but it wasn't so, was it? Was it, John?'

'This is not a subject to be discussed between a man and a woman.'

'We talked of it before. You confided in me before. John, I'm your sister.' She put her hand on his arm. 'For your own sake, and for Cousin Wenna's–'

'What has Wenna to do with any of this?'

'If it's in your mind to marry her one day, she will expect a normal married life,' Leah said steadily. 'You must be honest with yourself. John. Can you offer her that? Did you have it with Grace?'

'Not – completely.'

'And you still believe Teddy was your child?'

'I thought – I had no reason to think anything else,' he muttered.

'You mean you did not allow yourself to

304

consider any other possibility,' Leah said. 'But you must think of it now. Would Cousin Wenna be happy?'

'She wants children of her own,' he said dully. 'She wants babes.'

'And it seems that you could not give her children. You could not even–' Leah broke off and spread her hands wide.

'Teddy is – he was the one thing that was left out of my marriage,' John said. 'The one thing, Leah. Isn't it possible there is some mistake? There *are* seven month babes.'

'Teddy was a fine, strong child,' Leah said. 'It struck me as odd, but I dismissed it from my mind at the time. Now, it seems that we neither of us can dismiss it.'

'Wenna will expect children of her own,' John said. His face was deathly pale, whiter than it had been when he had learned of his wife's unfaithfulness.

'If you are truly fond of her,' Leah said, 'you will not offer her less than a complete relationship. It would not be fair, my dear.'

'No.' His shoulders drooping, he looked at her. 'No, it would not be fair to her, or any other woman.'

'Soon you will look at matters in a different light. You have the estate and your duties at the House.'

'It is not sufficient,' he said. 'Other men have desires as I have desires that they can satisfy. It is not sufficient.'

'You never complained before.'

'I had not met Wenna before,' he said.

'I can dismiss her, send her back to Wales. And Teddy – he need never know what we suspect.'

'What we know,' he corrected.

'Know,' Leah agreed. 'You still can claim Teddy as your own.'

'Teddy is Price's son,' John said. 'I can never look at him again without thinking that.'

'If only there was something, anything, I could do,' Leah said. 'I blame myself, you know. I tried to do what seemed best at the time and I failed.'

'No need to blame yourself,' John said. 'It's my failure. You tried to help and nobody can blame you for that.'

She would have said more, but he shook off her detaining hand and went out again into the hall. A moment later the front door slammed shut.

Beth, walking slowly up the drive, felt a brief lifting of her spirits. She had successfully evaded Leah's fussing and slipped out of the back door to catch a breath of free air.

At least she could be private in the grounds, with nobody to offer her hot drinks or remind her of the coming child if she began to cry.

Today however the urge to weep was less strong than usual. Spring had come and in spring Michael would come back. She was not sure how or why it was to happen, but she was so certain that it would that she was filled with a fierce impatience.

Somebody was galloping towards her. She raised her head and had a confused and blurred impression of John, crouched over the neck of his bay hunter. There was a look on her brother's face that reminded her of a picture she had once seen of a damned soul being thrust down into the flames. The expression changed as her brother saw her and tried to swerve. The horse, eager for exercise, reared and snorted and as Beth flung herself aside she heard the hard crack as John was unseated and hurled against a neighbouring oak.

It had happened before, she thought, struggling to her feet. Mam had stood on the steps as the men from the village carried Papa in.

'His horse must have stumbled as he took the jump. His neck is broken, Lady Margred.'

And Mam had said nothing, but her eyes had become dull and fixed, like the eyes of somebody dead. Like John's eyes, wide-open and staring, as he lay in the drive with the marks of the branches scored in weals across his face.

'John.' She whispered his name, but had she shouted it would have made no difference.

Nobody had come out from the courtyard. She would have to tell somebody, she supposed. but she could not think clearly. Her hands were cold and her back ached.

Abruptly she turned and began to run down the drive, away from the main house. There was nothing in her beyond the desire to run and, in running to blot out those nightmare seconds as the horse swerved and reared and John split his face against the oak.

She slowed down, panting, when she was some distance along the main road, but her legs continued to carry her forward, past the green shoots of corn in the meadows and the bridal lace of young apple blossom.

The little Post-Office, which was no more than an extra counter at the back of the village sweetshop was deserted save for Hattie Jenks who knitted her life away in the corner, occasionally rising with deep sighs to deal with any troublesome interruptions such as customers.

Her sigh, as Beth came in, was even more profound than usual. If Hattie Jenks, who was proud of being a good Christian woman, had her way the Falcons would have been driven lock, stock and barrel out of Marie Regina, except for poor Lord Falcon and Miss Leah who had been cruelly betrayed. On the other hand, a man who married a red-haired dancer might be said to have fallen into sin, and Miss Leah had been very foolish to wed a penniless nobody. On balance Hattie Jenks considered they had reaped a harvest of their own sowing. But there could be no doubt about Edith and Beth Falcon. Miss Edith had had the gall to bear a bastard child, and instead of dying in shame and poverty, as ladies in her situation always did in novels, she was living comfortably at Whittle Farm and had already been out on the tor with her babe in her arms.

As for Beth Falcon – Hattie Jenks averted her eyes from the bulging waistline of the girl's muslin dress and met an imploring stare from black-circled eyes. The chit had not even combed her hair and it straggled about her white face. How any man could have found her attractive was a mystery, but the one who had stayed at 'Witch's Dower' the previous summer had been an odd character. Forever stopping to sketch things on bits of paper, and Beth Falcon running around with him openly.

'I want to buy an envelope,' Beth said.

'Sixpence for six, Miss Falcon.'

'I only want one.'

'That'll be a penny,' Hattie Jenks slid it languidly across the counter.

'I've no money on me,' Beth said vaguely.

'I don't give credit,' Hattie Jenks began, and was stopped.

She was not certain afterwards what stopped her, but the other's gentle eyes were suddenly cold and hard, and the husky, hesitating voice was cool with generations of authority in it.

'You will give it to me,' was all that Beth said, but Hattie Jenks sat back trembling without another word.

Beth turned her back and slipped her moonstone into the envelope. Sealing it, she turned back to ask, in the same cool, authoritative tone, for pen, ink and stamp. They were produced in silence, 'as if,' Hattie Jenks said later, 'there was a spell on me!'

'You will see that this goes in the morning mail? It is of vital importance,' Beth said.

'Yes, Miss Falcon,' Hattie Jenks said, dry-mouthed. It was as Beth was leaving that she paused to give the news that Hattie Jenks would remember to the rest of her days; not so much for its content which was startling in itself, but for the dull, indifferent manner of its delivery.

'If you happen to see the Vicar,' Beth said, 'will you be good enough to tell him that my brother John has just been killed and is lying in our drive?'

The bell tinkled as she stepped into the street and began to climb the steep path that led up to the main road again. It would, she thought, all come right now. John was dead, and Price was in foreign land, and Paul Simmons had run away with Grace, but Michael was coming back to her.

Walking slowly, in the weariness of extreme shock, she crossed the road and went down the bridle path towards 'Witch's Dower'. She had not been there often during the winter and the little house had a neglected air.

The front door had swollen with the damp and required a hard push before it would open, and there was a fine film of dust over the tables and chairs. If Michael came now nothing would be ready for him.

She found the broom and began to sweep, the dust rising into her nose and eyes and making her cough. If Michael came now he would be amused and tease her for her untidiness.

Some part of her mind knew that he would not yet arrive for he had not yet received the moonstone, so there was really plenty of time to prepare for him. But if he had needed her she would have known it before any message was sent.

Her back was aching intolerably, each spasm rising to a crescendo and then dying down for a few minutes.

The cottage looked better now. Beth gave a final polish to the table and bit her lip under a fresh onslaught of pain. She would feel more comfortable she decided, if she went outside and sat down.

She was surprised, when she pulled open the front door again, to see that it was already quite dim in the clearing. She would need to light the lamp soon or Michael might lose his way in the darkness. But first she would rest for a while. As she lowered herself to the grass there was the gushing of water between her legs and then the pain began again, sharper than before.

At Kingsmead Leah mourned, dry-eyed and erect. One of the farm hands had found John and run to bring the news. The Vicar, summoned by a garbled message from Hattie Jenks, had been and gone. The lamps had been lit, and John's body laid in the drawing-room to await the attention of the undertakers on the following day.

Leah crossed the room and sat down, her eyes fixed upon the shrouded form. It was terrible to realize that she would never talk to John again, never advise or guide him. He had been her favourite brother.

There was no sign of Beth. She had probably sneaked off to visit Edith or Cousin Wenna. On the whole Leah was not too sorry. She had no desire for intruders upon her mourning time. It was brief enough in all conscience for soon there would be business matters to deal with and the funeral to arrange. At least, by dying young, he had been spared the misery of another unhappy marriage. Wenna would not have been a suitable wife for him. She would have interfered and tried to steal away Teddy's affection.

Edith, rocking Cal to sleep in the parlour of Whittle Farm, thought of Paul Simmons with fierce hatred. She no longer wished to tell anybody the name of her son's father. In the long winter months she had concentrated on remembering how, while he was promising to elope with her, he had been seducing Grace. Now there was room in her heart only for her child. She brooded over the cradle with passionate intensity. Cal would have everything she could provide for him, everything except a father, but she would make certain that he never felt the lack of one.

Wenna checked for the third time that the slates were in place ready for the next morning's lessons.

She had felt restless all day, though there was no reason for it.

It must, she decided, have been the interview with John that had unsettled her. She was fond of her cousin and, with time, she was certain that her feelings would become stronger and deeper, but the prospect of becoming Lady Falcon was not one of unmixed pleasure. It would mean sharing a house with Cousin Leah and giving up the school. It would mean marrying a divorced man, which would shock many people, though Wenna paid small heed to public opinion.

She began to mount the stairs to her apartment, and, as suddenly, turned and came down again. It was almost dark and had become much cooler, but the notion of taking a walk had leapt into her mind. She pulled her cloak from its hook and wrapped it about herself.

For a reason she couldn't understand the woods across the river beckoned her. She had seldom walked in them, preferring the open fields, but on this evening she strode purposefully down the long, curving drive, and turned right in the main drive towards the bridge. In a few moments, without understanding why, she began to run down the bridle path.

CHAPTER SEVENTEEN

'We have a great deal to thank you for, Cousin Wenna,' Leah said.

'It was pure chance that took me to the cottage,' Wenna said.

'If you had not found them she and the child would have both been dead by the morning.'

'The babe is healthy enough now at all events.'

'But very tiny. She will need special care for several months. Beth too.'

'You look tired,' Wenna said, regarding the other's drawn face. 'I wish I could do something to help you.'

'You're very kind,' Leah said. 'but I must learn to shoulder my burdens alone. If John had lived – I hoped so much that you and he might–'

'We had talked of it,' Wenna said briefly.

'Now I must think of Teddy and of my own little Mary. Lord Edward Falcon sounds very grand for a baby.'

'And of Beth's child.'

'Poor little mite. She has insisted on calling it Levanah,' Leah said. 'It means child of the moon, I believe. Beth always had such odd notions.'

'I saw Cousin Edith at the funeral,' Wenna said.

'At least she didn't come to the church,' Leah said.

'At least she didn't do that. But the child – was the child with her?'

'Cal? Yes, wrapped in a shawl.'

'To bring a tiny creature out into the air so few weeks after its birth,' Leah said. 'Edith never had any sense. I tremble for that poor child!'

'There is, I suppose, no possibility of a reconciliation?'

'None,' Leah said. Her face had grown hard and still. 'I will never forgive Edith for shaming us all.'

'Beth—'

'Is an entirely different matter. Beth is hardly more than a child. She has always been a strange, dreamy girl. I am convinced the man forced her and she will not admit it.'

'And the father,' Wenna thought, 'was not your husband. That is what you cannot forgive.'

'I ought to be going. There is still school to be opened tomorrow morning.'

'Life must go on,' Leah said wryly.

For a moment Wenna's lips were compressed with pain. Then she touched Leah's hand briefly and went out.

'Life must go on,' Leah said again and made an impatient little gesture as if she were brushing away grief. There were three children at Kingsmead now, and it was her task to care for them. Tenderness possessed her as she dwelled upon each one in turn.

John's child, for nobody must ever know

that Price was his father, was a sturdy child, just beginning to walk. He would need firm discipline later if he were not to become impossibly demanding.

Mary was a pretty baby with a fuzz of dark hair. When Leah thought of her daughter her eyes misted a little. She had not believed that she could feel such passion for so small a being.

There remained Beth's child, the oddly named Levanah. At a week old she was the tiniest and most frail of the three, with a mark on her thigh like a crescent moon, and eyes that slanted up at the corners and were a clear, pale amber in colour. In a curious way Leah felt more drawn to this baby than to either of the others.

Thinking of Levanah, she drew from the writing desk the letter that had arrived earlier in the day. She had opened it, and its contents had occupied her mind during the funeral service. Now she read it again.

Dearest Beth,

Your ring reached me as an answer to long months of wondering if you still felt about me as I feel about you. I even tried to forget you, but that was impossible. Oh, my dear, I am more than twice your age, but with you

I feel young again. It was with such joy that I received the moonstone, for it means that you have as much need of me as I have of you.

Darling, my wife died quite suddenly three weeks ago. I didn't love her, but there was affection between us once, and I felt a certain regret when she had gone. An emptiness too, because I was not certain if you still loved me. But the moonstone gives me great hope.

Now when I come to you, I will be able to offer marriage. I have resigned my position at the bank and have enough for the two of us to live modestly for a year or so, while I try to establish myself as a portrait painter. I have little to offer you, my love, but one day you will be proud of me. I promise it.

The final sale of my house and contents is under way. Give me one week, sweetheart, and I will be with you, and this time we will both step into the dream.

Your devoted,

Michael.

It was a good letter. Leah wished that Beth could be allowed to read it, but that would mean Beth's being allowed to leave Kingsmead. She would go away with this Michael

Shaw, and they would take Levanah with them. That yellow-eyed scrap, with the crescent moon on her thigh, would be reared somewhere away from Marie Regina. That beautiful Falcon child would be reared by a dreaming girl and an elderly man.

Sometimes it was necessary to be cruel in order to be kind. Leah folded the letter away and locked it into the narrow, secret drawer at the back of the dresser. The moonstone she held in her hand. It was cool, its milky surface flashed with palest lilac. She had always liked the ring.

Mounting the stairs in her rustling black gown, the mourning veil turned back over her smoothly brushed hair, Leah was an elegant and tragic figure. Annie, coming through from the kitchen with a shovelful of coals, gazed after her in admiration. One trouble after another and Miss Leah weathered them all.

Beth was propped against pillows in the bed where she had slept since childhood. Nearby Levanah slept peacefully in a carved wooden cradle. Sunlight, falling across the bed, brought out the reddish gleams in Beth's hair.

She looked up from the book she was reading as Leah came in and asked, as she had asked every day since her child had been born:

'Is there anything in the mail for me?'

'Are you feeling better?' Leah evaded the question and sat down in the chair by the bed.

'Much better. I wish I could get up. *Is* there any mail for me?'

'You've asked that every day. You know letters only come weekly.'

'But it is a week since – never mind! There's tomorrow.'

'I have been wondering,' Leah pulled the chair nearer, 'if it might not be a good idea for you to go away for a few weeks. Aunt Catrin would be glad to have a visitor, I'm sure.'

'Go up to Wales? But surely the baby is too little to travel?'

'I wasn't proposing to pack you off today,' Leah said. 'In a month or two, when you're stronger – you could leave the baby here. We'll have to get a wet-nurse anyway. You're not producing sufficient milk, and I haven't enough for two babies. You'd trust her to me while you were on holiday, wouldn't you?'

'Yes, of course. You're marvellous with babies.'

'Perhaps we could close the school for a

month and, Cousin Wenna could travel with you. The change would do her good too.'

'I don't really want to go to Wales,' Beth said. 'I'd much rather stay here. I'm expecting somebody, you see.'

'Oh, my dear!' Leah rose abruptly and went over to the window.

'I know he'll come,' Beth said. 'I'm sorry if you disapprove, and I have tried to go on without him, but it isn't any use. We're part of each other. I feel so strongly that he'll come – Leah, what is it? Why do you look at me like that?'

'You sent your moonstone ring to him.'

'To the bank where he works. Leah, how did?– I wish you would tell me what's happened. Is it Michael? Has he written to me? Don't be angry, Leah. I know he has a wife, but a marriage without love is no marriage at all.'

'There was a letter. The ring was enclosed.' Leah opened her hand to reveal the pale, gleaming stone in its thin circlet of gold.

'A letter? Is he coming soon?' Beth's face was flushed with eagerness. 'Surely you didn't open my letter?'

'The letter was addressed to me.'

'To you? Michael wrote to you?'

'Not Michael Shaw. His employer – oh Beth, I hoped you wouldn't ask. I wanted to spare you.' Leah's face twitched violently; her fingers tightened tremblingly on the moonstone.

'What's happened?' Beth whispered. 'Leah, tell me. *Leah?*'

'They wrote saying that Mr Shaw had died very suddenly three weeks ago.'

'It's not true,' said Beth. The colour had fled from her face and her eyes stared at unimaginable horror.

'He must have had a premonition,' Leah said sorrowfully. 'He told one of his colleagues that if anything happened to him, and if a moonstone ring was sent, it was to be returned to me at this address. I believe he truly cared for you. Beth.'

'I know he did,' Beth said.

'I wish I could have brought you good news,' Leah said. 'With all my heart I wish it. But you have the baby. You will find that children are a great comfort.'

'Yes.' Beth looked without interest at the cradle.

'And a holiday with Aunt Catrin – Wenna says that the mountains are beautiful in summer. You could go within a few days; we could pay for a private compartment on the train. My dear, I would do anything in the world to help you.'

'I know,' Beth said. 'I know, but I want to be by myself now. Please, Leah, let me be by myself for a little while.'

'Have a good cry,' Leah advised. 'One always feels much better after a good cry. Remember that he loved you, and that time heals all griefs.'

'But I don't want to cry,' Beth thought with faint surprise. 'I don't want to cry at all.'

She pushed back the bedcovers and swung her legs over the side. She was regaining her strength rapidly, but her reflection in the mirror was that of a frail, white-faced girl in the high necked, lace trimmed nightdress that made her look much younger than her nineteen years.

'Michael is dead,' she said to the girl in the mirror, 'Michael is dead.'

She walked slowly to the cradle and looked down at the tiny shrouded form, its limbs wrapped tightly in a lacy shawl, its eyes tightly screwed up against the light.

'Levanah,' she said aloud, but the name meant nothing and the child was no longer part of her.

A darkness swept over her that was like no

darkness she had ever known. It gripped her spirit, holding it fast in a place where hope was unknown. Somewhere beyond the darkness Michael was waiting for her. She could not breathe properly because she was weighed down in her own body, imprisoned in flesh.

Moving very slowly, Beth went over to the dressing table and picked up the little silver penknife that John had given her some years before. It dazzled her eyes as she turned it in her fingers, but the darkness didn't go away. Even the room was growing dimmer as if the blackness inside her were spreading out to cover the world.

She drew the sharp point of the little knife across her blue veined wrists, and watched with an almost detached interest as the red blood spurted out, down the white nightdress. There had been pain but it was blurring in her mind and the darkness was lifting, fading into silver grey.

There was a whirling inside her and a thin silver cord stretched between her and the small figure huddled on the carpet. She was calling for Michael, but she was alone in the greyness and a part of her knew, with sudden and blinding certainty, that she had come too soon. The cord was stretched to its limits. It would break soon and then she would be trapped in the grey mist that was worse than the blackness. If somebody would come she could get back again. She wanted to go back because Michael wasn't here.

'Shall I take Miss Beth her coffee now?' Annie enquired of Leah, pausing in the kitchen doorway.

'Not yet. She's sleeping. Make a fresh cup in about an hour and take it to her then,' Leah instructed.

Coffee was bad for nursing mothers but Beth had always had a passion for it.

Leah watched Annie go back into the kitchen. The house was silent, the babies still asleep, though Teddy was outgrowing his afternoon nap and would soon be demanding attention again. He would be like Price in character.

That reminded her that she must write to Price, telling him what had happened. She would have to put the facts very carefully lest it enter his head that Teddy might be his child.

When she had written to Price she would drive over to the school and ask Wenna how she felt about paying a surprise visit to Saron Farm.

Beth was recovering quickly from her ordeal, and several months in the mountains would complete her return to full health. It would also help to heal her grief, for it was obvious that she had believed herself in love with the wretched man. Perhaps she had better look in at Beth just for a moment. By now the poor child would be past her first crying and she would be grateful for consolation.

Leah went back up the stairs and walked slowly along the gallery towards her sister's room. The portraits gazing out indifferently from their frames, were part of her heritage and she scarcely bothered to glance at them. It was the future that mattered, and the future had been entrusted to her.

Late afternoon sunshine mellowed the pastel-shaded apartment. In the cradle Levanah was still sleeping, making the little sneezing noises emitted by the newly born. Beth was sitting on the floor, her back leaning against the bed, her head bent.

'Beth? Beth?'

Leah advanced a few steps into the room and stood, transfixed, her eyes fixed upon the dark-stained nightdress and carpet.

'Beth?' Leah stopped, putting her hand under her sister's chin.

Beth's eyelids flickered and her lips moved. The blood running from her wrists was flowing more sluggishly, its scarlet stream thickening and darkening. There was still time.

'Darling, I'll get help,' Leah said. 'I'll get help.' She rose and hurried out, past the silent, staring portraits, along the gallery to the head of the stairs. Lists flew through her mind. Tourniquets – one of the farm hands had gashed an artery on a sickle once and she had applied a tourniquet. Clean linen, alcohol to prevent infection, raw liver and red wine and onions – onions were marvellous for increasing the blood. If Beth died...

If Beth died, there would be no need to lie to Michael Shaw. There would be no need to pretend. Lies and pretence were hateful. They were against her nature.

If Beth died, there would be another child for Leah to bring up. Not that she expected to do everything by herself. She would probably send them to Cousin Wenna to be educated. That would set a good example to the village. There had been so much scandal that it would take a long time to make people forget.

Poor Beth had always been a strange girl.

Strange and dreamy, with no sense of morals. There was no guarantee that if she lived she would not fall prey to the next smooth tongued gentleman who came along, and bring more disgrace upon the family.

At the foot of the stairs Leah hesitated, and then walked through into the solar. She had to think. There was no sense in rushing into anything. She had rushed before and it had turned out badly.

All her adult life, ever since she had realized with a thrill of disgust, that her parents had been lovers before their marriage, and that she had been conceived out of wedlock, she had pushed the knowledge down deeply so deeply that she thought she had forgotten. It rose up now to mock her.

But even bad judgement could be turned to good account. It had been foolish to imagine that she could turn Price's mistress into John's wife, but Teddy was a fine boy. Even her telling John the truth which had led to his frantic gallop meant that Wenna had been saved from an unhappy marriage.

A new book from the big London bookshop where she ordered novels and periodicals was on the table. She had opened it the previous day and glanced through it with a contemptuous smile. 'House Valiant' by Paul Simmons was, after all her fears, no more than an indifferently written romance with nothing in it to reveal the truth behind the fiction.

Even her marriage to Paul had been a good thing in the end. It had revealed Edith's treachery and rid Kingsmead of Grace, and there was Mary to prove that Leah too had known the touch of a man.

She picked up the book, ran her fingers over the lettering and laid it down again. That episode was at an end. No sense in remembering. After a moment she sat down at the desk, quill poised over a fresh sheet of paper. Her hand was shaking and there were tears in her eyes, but she forced herself to write steadily:

Dear Mr Shaw,
It is with the deepest regret that I write to inform you...

Over Kingsmead the sun glowed for a last defiant moment as it sank below the trees, and a grey twilight enveloped Marie Regina. Deep in the woods a vixen deprived of her mate, howled bitterness to the faint outlines of an indifferent moon. A moth pattered against a window pane disturbing a little shower of moisture from a trailing creeper.

Within the bedroom Levanah stirred in her cradle and whimpered as if some phantom disturbed her sleep, but the scarlet-stained figure huddled nearby made no move.

In the solar Leah continued to write her letter.

1892

EPILOGUE

The woods were a glory of bluebells, and the day so warm that little spirals of golden dust rose up from the road and sank down again.

In the meadow beyond the churchyard, near to the weather-beaten stone that marked the last resting place of the Falcon wife drowned as a witch, a man stood, hat in hand, looking down at another grave. He had guessed where it would be, but seeing it brought him no peace.

'Elizabeth Falcon'
1870 – 1889

The stone cross with its bleak inscription was all that remained. There was nothing for him here, and he had not the heart to call at Kingsmead or make enquiries in the village.

Bitter regret twisted his face for a moment, and few would have recognized the calmly smiling, rather shy man whose disturbing and compelling paintings were attracting increasingly high prices in the European galleries.

There were children playing in the cemetery. He could hear their shrill voices and could see their small figures.

They intruded upon his grief, reminding him that he, who was deeply fond of children, had no child of his own. Without reading the inscription again he turned away and, remounting his horse, rode slowly back in the direction of the London road.

From the church a voice called.

'Children! We're going home now. Come and say good-afternoon to the Vicar!'

Two of them obeyed at once scampering over the grassy mounds, the fair-haired boy pulling the dark-haired child in the pink dress. The third, a tiny girl with straight, light red hair cut in bangs above slanting, yellowish eyes toddled after them more slowly.

'You must not make such a noise in the churchyard,' Leah said, coming out into the porch as the children rounded the corner of the building. 'It is disrespectful. Now Levanah, take your thumb out of your mouth and make your curtsey. You too, Mary. Teddy, little gentlemen shake hands without scowling.'

'They are a credit to your training, ma'am,' the Vicar said heartily.

'My cousin, Mrs Davies, will share that responsibility when Teddy starts school with her in the autumn,' Leah said.

'A splendid woman Mrs Davies.'

'A most satisfactory teacher,' Leah agreed. 'What is it, Levanah?'

'I seen my Papa,' the child said.

'"Saw", not "seen",' Leah bent to straighten her niece's hair-ribbon. 'And you didn't, darling. Your papa is in Heaven.'

'I seen my Papa,' Levanah said obstinately.

'She greets every gentleman she meets as her Papa,' Leah said ruefully. 'I wish it were possible to satisfy her.'

'The children are fortunate in having you,'

the Vicar said.

'I do my best.' Leah straightened her narrow shoulders, her eyes clear and gentle.

There was another fatherless child growing up at Whittle Farm on the other side of the monastery ruins. Her heart yearned towards him, but her mouth was patient.

'You set an example to us all,' the Vicar bowed.

'It is no virtue in me,' she disclaimed modestly. 'I am not denying that I have my faults, but nobody will ever be able to say that I am not devoted to my family.'

This Large Print Book, for people
who cannot read normal print,
is published under the auspices of

THE ULVERSCROFT FOUNDATION

THE FALCON AND
THE MOON